Modus Vivendi

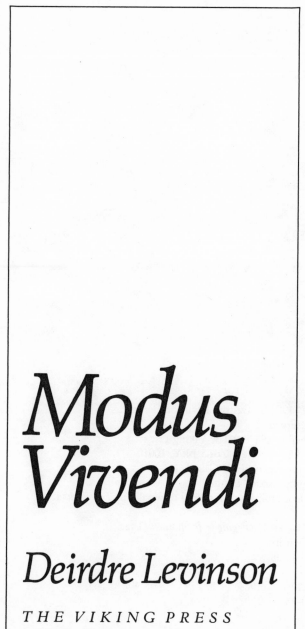

Modus Vivendi

Deirdre Levinson

THE VIKING PRESS
NEW YORK

Copyright © 1984 by Deirdre Levinson Bergson
All rights reserved
First published in 1984 by The Viking Press
40 West 23rd Street, New York, N.Y. 10010
Published simultaneously in Canada by
Penguin Books Canada Limited
A selection from this book appeared originally in *The Raritan.*

Library of Congress Cataloging in Publication Data
Levinson, Deirdre.
  Modus vivendi.
  I. Title.
PS3562.E9214M6 1984   813'.54   83-40246
ISBN 0-670-48404-0

Printed in the United States of America
Set in Linotron Bembo
Designed by Ann Gold

TO ALLEN

Modus Vivendi

I'm back at school again. I have to teach the great works again—those aesthetic phenomena which alone, according to Nietzsche, make existence still bearable for us. But I am at a loss now what to say about those works. I will open my mouth and my tongue will stiffen, I will stand there dumbstruck, snorting, impotent. I consulted McNulty about this. McNulty and I ride to school together. We each lost an infant son within the same week, something over a year ago. I took off school for that year, but McNulty went right on teaching. McNulty isn't a communicative man, but he tries: we both try. I want a badge to wear on my naked forehead, to account for me in the time of trouble when I stand there pinioned, lockjawed, mammering. Veteran McNulty, though, favors direct encounter—just occasionally, only momentarily, tempting the tidal wave, putting one toe in (so to speak), testing, testing. He says it isn't so bad, just an awkward couple of minutes' silence. As for with what, other than silence, one is to encompass that silence, "Pavlov lives," McNulty avers. "Bell rings, students assemble, teacher teaches. In conditioned reflex we trust!"

I know about McNulty's conditioned reflexes though. One of his last year's students told me they were half-hours on end his couple of minutes' silences. But he's back in the living stream again now, in the wake of a girl. His divorce is through, his next marriage imminent: they've bought a brass bed and the wedding ring already. The creature hath a purpose, and his eyes are bright with it. He chairs a seditious campus committee twice weekly after classes, in which my participation would be most welcome. But I have to go straight home after classes to lie down. I can't hold out for the length of a day. When I hear myself talking that way I could retch; but I'm bound to explain myself, my non-self. I can't stop explaining. When my colleagues pause on the wing for a civil how-are-you, I freely give tongue, nothing extenuate. I'm at no loss what to say then; there's no rivaling this apologist pro vita sua on that subject. I'm not my old self these days, as you see; I have to go armed to my classes with wrench and crowbar, yerking at the texts like a thrall on an assembly line. Grind, grind, grind, on thy cold gray stone, O nose. I'm grinding to a halt. I can't make it to the next class. I consulted Mrs. Gorodetsky about this. When she was widowed in mid-semester four years ago, she didn't take off school for more than a week. I sought to compare notes with her on exhaustion pursuant to bereavement. She jumped. "Why? Who have you lost?" I could see, when I reminded her, she didn't take it kindly that I'd equalized our losses. I could understand that. I wouldn't myself have dreamt, before Toto's death, that the loss of so short-lived a being could cause such wholesale devastation. I couldn't till then— though it was only from him that I'd learnt how much, how most I liked a benign countenance, how exactly he was what I'd wanted—I couldn't till then have guessed at the size of the capital investment. "Better now than later,"

said one of the doctors at Toto's deathbed, with intent to
console me. But I don't know about that. There was so
much in him already. How long must a life be to be ac-
counted a life, and by what gauge does one measure the
love invested in it? Still, I don't have any patent on suffering; I hold no commission in the ranks of the bereaved. I
had Eli, I had Poppy. The night Toto died, when I took
stock of what was left to sustain me, I thought, There's always talking to Eli. I should have begged Mrs. Gorodetsky's pardon.

There was Eli, there was Poppy; there was, preemi-
nently, the pursuit of compensation. Toto hadn't been dead
two days before we were back at Dr. Feffer's office. Indeed, we had this errand in mind even while he still had
some hours of life to go, such is the nature of true need.
Feffer said, "No, you haven't come too soon. My advice to
you is to have another child at once. You've got none of the
obstetrical hazards we often find in women of, excuse me,
your age. So it was a coarcted aorta, eh? Terrific blood
pressure. There's nothing I or anyone else can say to console you in this verfuckte world. All that showed up in the
baby's cardiograph at birth was a heart murmur. If we kept
every baby born with a heart murmur in the hospital,
they'd be ten deep in the corridors. I know what you're
going through. You can't hope for consolation. That's the
way of this vercackte world. As your obstetrician, I recommend that you set about having another child at once.
You can have the next one on the house."

Since then, every morning on waking in this dark world
and wide, I reach for the thermometer, and measure, and
note the result on the graph provided. We wait for the day
it rises sharply, and do exactly as we're told. But still no
sign, though a second autumn is under way, and I have to
be back at school again, to stand up in front of those rows

of faces, and hour by hour proclaim my vacuity, and day by day endure that disgrace.

Last time I was standing there I was pregnant—not much less incompetent, no less terrified. I don't know which tortures me more now, the unbearable difference or the unbearable likeness: sometimes one, sometimes the other. The fog moved in in the first month of pregnancy, right into the cortex, and settled like lead. I taught through those nine months, mostly stupefied, always exhausted. I counted. Week by week, day by day, class by class, I counted those nine months away. My relief, my diversion, my mind's sole voluntary activity was counting. Stairs to the classroom, steps across the campus, stops in the subway, floors in the elevator, people in line in the supermarket, I was counting towards the day I could lie in the hospital and stare at the ceiling, the dull frightful panic over, no classes, nothing to get through, nothing to wish away. Till the day Toto was born I didn't stop counting. He was no sooner dead than I was at it again. Excepting those few weeks of his life, I've been counting incessantly for two years now. Counting forward from menses to ovulation, ovulation to menses, backwards to the months of his maturation, his birthday, his death day, I counted last year away. I've got all that and more to count now I'm back at school again—the classes, the days, the weeks to count till the semester's over and the next one begins.

I have to keep counting, have to keep moving. His kind, alert dark eyes: in the last days of his life the muscles atrophied. They stuck tape over them; they took off the tape. His eyes had rolled inward, crossed ferociously. I have to get from my office, across the campus, into the classroom, recite my notes, out of the classroom, back to counting. For a moment sometimes I think, I'm counting away my only life. I think, My *life*! Then I think, My life? What about *his* life? Let me out. Let me be fatally mugged in the subway, stabbed in the dark street, get it over with quickly. I did what I did. I know what I did. I've lived for nearly a year with it.

I go over and over the first weeks of that pregnancy— the weeks in which I dealt him his deathblow. I alter the past. What I made happen I make unhappen. I devise an unending variety of alternative ways I could have taken to the way I did take. To this end, in concocting diverse means by which I might have ensured my absence from school for the first trimester of that pregnancy, my ingenuity is inexhaustible. If I'd had contrivance enough to have broken an ankle, or to have persuaded Feffer to recommend my absence; if there'd been a general strike; if we'd borrowed the money; if we'd won the state lottery; if I'd just said I couldn't keep going; if I'd just not gone.

But I did say I couldn't keep going. I first said so to Feffer. I told him I couldn't combat the torpor, and begged him for stimulants. He said to wait until the first trimester was well over, Christmastime. That left me with a hundred and four class periods to get through unaided, to endure hour by hour a hundred and four times over the reflection of my idiot image in my audience's restless, disgusted, bored eyes. I thought I could not outlive the shame of it. Mornings I rose, counting: forty-six more schooldays, a hundred and four more teaching hours till Christmas. Breakfast for Poppy. Pack sandwich, fill flask for lunch. Only forty-six more times till Christmas I'll be filling this flask. Into the bus with Poppy. Out of the bus, cross the road, up the street. "Be a monster, Mama, and chase after me." Only forty-six more times till Christmas being a monster, a no-good monster, too tired to chase. "When will you not be too tired, Mama?" That's the memory she'll have of her early-childhood mother, al-

ways-tired mother, no-fun mother. From Poppy's school,
forward to mine. Into the subway. Forty-six more out-
bound journeys, just counting till Christmas. A hundred
and six more till summer. It will never be over. It will be
over. On that final homebound journey from school, this
torture all ended, my joy will be uncontainable. My disgrace will be uncontainable. Enough of that. Turn to the
ads. What have they to offer? A career in the army. You
bet. Drilling, saluting, polishing, rallying the ranks,
sweeping up the barracks:

> *"I'd ask no nights off when the bustle's over,*
> *Enjoying so the dirt."*

Out of the subway, on to the bus. If I could just sit in this
bus till it were all over. Off the bus, quick march down the
little suburban wintry street. If it were spring now, I'd
smell the lilacs, first the purple, then the white, sniff up
the scent against the day's levy. How faintly they smell
though, in America, indistinctly, even in full bloom—no-
where in the running with English lilacs. But it may be in
me, that attenuation: that's failing too, the keenest of my
senses. When I was a child—in postwar England, when
food was short, and shopkeepers were concealing their
caches from all but their favorites—I would stick my head
out the window of a morning and identify authoritatively,
from miles across town, what edible cargo was come into
dock. I could stand at the crossroads of any town and,
through the heaviest barrage of urban fumes, nose my way
through a maze of streets to the oranges. Oranges are one
thing: I've met my rivals for oranges; but I could track
down apples with no less exactitude. When it comes to apples, I've never met my equal. Smoking is taking its toll
there, however. Chain-smoking through classes, a ciga-

rette dangling from every finger, I sit like a sacrifice on a self-made pyre, behind clouds of smoke never dense enough to dissociate my diminished head from the clouds of verbiage emitted by it. Not the public disgrace, but having to toil for it, is my torment. Fetch forth the stocks, put in my legs: under no compulsion there to annul myself, composed, self-contained, let me sit there till summer.

At my desk in the lunch hour, the afternoon class awaiting me like the rack, I dream of a hold-up in the classroom. Summarily dismissing the students, I grapple unto my soul the armed intruder, my salvation, bless him, the means to my long hospitalization, to lying there till summer, just staring at the ceiling, this hell all ended. I ask nothing more.

Class time. No way out. Cross the campus, head down. Head down, burble the hour away; wiped out, trudge back to my office, sit there till my evening class, cold, starving; too tired to make the journey to the cafeteria; smoke the hunger away; wash my mouth out at the drinking fountain; smoke more. Can't meet the evening class. Call it off. Called it off twice already in the past month. Too tired, anyway, to cross the campus again to pin a notice on the classroom door. Don't call it off then, just don't turn up. Too tired to go home. Stand up now, put on your coat, pack up your briefcase, forward to the bus stop, on the bus, off the bus, into the subway, on to the train, eighteen stops, count them; change trains, and again, five stops more; off the train, up the steps, twenty-seven steps, count them; into the building, into the elevator, twelve floors up; key ready, key in door, home. I cut my evening class, again. I can't go on.

I said so to Eli. But it was like calling for help in a dream: eyes have they, but they see not; they have ears, but they hear not. He was up for tenure that year. Failing that, he was finished—bereft of vocation, livelihood, at his age, in his field, in such parlous times—closed out everywhere. Still, we had our priorities: this was no accidental pregnancy. I said I couldn't take Poppy to school and fetch her home and mind her at weekends and cook and shop and wash and write weekly to both sets of parents, and prepare for classes and travel three hours a day and teach full-time plus overtime. I said I couldn't do everything, I had to lie down. One doesn't endear oneself to a man in trammels by itemizing his neglected obligations. I said, "I can't go on." He was holding a coat hanger in his hands. He snapped it in two. "If you can't, you can't" was all he said.

So I did go on. We couldn't pay the rent, couldn't pay what we owed to date on Poppy's nursery-school fees, if I didn't go on. Two salaries weren't enough to stop the hole in our bank account, let alone one. I couldn't take off school, short of Eli's insistence. Our debts were legion as it was: I couldn't add to them, not without his insistence. I couldn't bear him to think of me as a burden. I couldn't bear that shame, couldn't bear the other; so I bore neither.

It said in the book, the little outdated pregnancy book, that there was no evidence that pep pills could injure the fetus. The other book, the up-to-date one, warned against taking any drugs, in the first trimester especially, not prescribed by the doctor. Feffer wouldn't prescribe; but I had my little stock of them, got from unofficial sources, hoarded away for emergencies. The book said there was no evidence. Thus I got through the hundred hours. I sat at my desk in school, pitched in despair. I thought, I am risking this little one's life by swallowing this pill; and I swallowed the pill. There's nothing easier than swallowing a pill. The book said there was no evidence. Every day at school I swallowed a pill. I called Feffer again. I said that without medication I could not do my work. Only two more weeks, he replied, then I'd be across the danger line, then he'd prescribe. Every schoolday for two more weeks I swallowed a pill. When I was safe, then he prescribed, and as soon as it was safe I forgot that once it had not been so; and not till months after Toto's death did I remember, would I remember, though he signaled distress soon enough from the womb. In the fourth month I bled, but for no more than a day. That isn't an uncommon phenomenon in pregnancy. In the fifth month I was sent to Slansky for testing.

Slansky interprets the findings from the prenatal tests they run on expectant women of advanced age. They stick a hollow needle in your belly, safe-conducted by a videotape recording sights and sounds within. So I saw the outline of my son's head four months before he was born, and I heard the sounds of the elements he inhabited there; and it was amazing: it was Wordsworth's immortal sea; Lear on the heath, hurricanoes drenching steeples; a great noise of waters. A month later Slansky telephoned the results to me at school. My office is situated in what is known as the bullpen. The noise there is conspicuously devoid of any resemblance to those sounds in great Nature with which the poets are wont to associate the unconquerable mind of man. There are neither doors nor windows, neither privacy nor ventilation there. I once reminded my departmental chairman that persons in my condition customarily required oxygen, and wondered aloud whether I should sue the college. He sent a memorandum to the administration, which came to rest in a wastepaper basket in an air-conditioned office. So I took Slansky's call on my back, gasping. "No aberrations discoverable from the cells harvested," he said, "but after three weeks the entire cell culture died. Unprecedented in our experience. No knowing what it means. You can risk it and take the consequences, or you can have an abortion. It's up to you."

I said I'd risk it.

"I'm glad," Slansky replied gloomily. "Please call us when you're in labor. We'd like to know what happens. Your case is unique. Did you say you wanted to know the child's sex?"

I said, Given such a prognosis, I certainly didn't.

"Ah, yes, well, it's a boy," Slansky sighed. "Remember, if you change your mind and decide on an abortion, we can give you one up till the end."

I said I wouldn't change my mind.

"Good," he concluded sadly, "but remember you have been forewarned."

That same day Eli's department voted in favor of his tenure, subject necessarily to the whim of the higher administration. Thus, respectively forewarned, we toiled each through our days. I scarcely dwelt on Slansky's forewarning; never thought to account for it. All I knew was that I had to get through those classes, and all Eli knew was that he had to get tenure. Nightly by the hour he reviewed his chances, nightly concluding with an extenuating salute to our priorities so frankly mechanical that I winced for him. Once, when I asked him, taking him unawares in the midst of a prolonged overview of his chances, if anything mattered more than tenure, he demanded, indignant and startled, to know what *could* matter more.

But the impenetrable fog in my head, if not the fatigue, had cleared somewhat by then. I never stopped counting, but I could simulate my assertive, sententious old self by then, teach with a modicum of competence again. Of the classes I was assigned that spring semester there was one —friendly, merry, cooperative, literate—of a kind best sorting with far-off, far happier teaching days, yet still sporadically extant. Shakespeare's Sonnets were our texts, love and time our themes, the imminent finale of both our discussion.

"Inasmuch," I said, "as we are undoubtedly among the last representatives of the posterity that wears this world out till the ending doom—for this world (putative nuclear disarmament notwithstanding) is now well and truly worn out; the ecologists say it can no longer sustain us (ten million of our species will perish in the forthcoming year by famine alone)—and inasmuch as it must follow that even the poet's pow'rful rhyme, eternal lines, black ink, virtue of pen cannot outlive all life, it behooves us, as among his last readers, therefore to read him well."

An outraged class, in the name of their champion jouncing for them *in utero*, unanimously impugned my credibility and good faith. "Am I," I replied undaunted, "because the imminent close-out of the species is a fact, to be therefore an accomplice before the fact? Not I. Just one last shot in the arm for posterity; one last heaving of the brick against the ending doom; one last participant in what remains of life's feast; one last reader of the great works."

I could not bear the thought of meeting those students again after Toto's death, after I got notice of what it was to behold the ending doom. I saw then with unprecedented clarity, beyond the menace and misery of the world we inhabit, its beauty, its vastness, its immense possibilities that my little son would never attempt. I saw how marvelous it was, this world, whose imminent end I had not mourned, how precious the species whose doom I had made light of, and I couldn't bear the thought of meeting those students again. At the end of the semester they had given me stamped self-addressed postcards with blank spaces to be filled in with the child's date of birth and sex and name. At the end of that semester too Eli's tenure recommendation was rejected, his racking suspense over and done with; so we were freed, Eli and I, simultaneously, each from our solitary unheeding bondage, and returned to the world as our son entered it.

I remember the moment, that sunlit, incomparably jolly moment when Feffer moved up from his ministrations at the foot of the bed to snarl in my ear, "It's a boy, as you know, and he's normal. So much for that prick Slansky!" Then I heard Eli's unmistakable, vulnerable footsteps crashing through the corridor, and his deafening voice calling me. "He needn't think," he said without humor, contemplating the preternaturally bright, sharp mien of his son, "that he's going to push his sister around." But then he saw how benign those alert wide eyes were, how exquisite his long slender fingers, how the tenderness of his spirit informed the knowing face and the tall hairy little man's body, and was satisfied. As for me, I saw all posterity vindicated in that baby.

The pediatrician came to look him over, and detected a heart murmur, but nothing to worry about. Poppy had been born with a heart murmur too that had never given cause for a moment's alarm. So we took him home on the fourth day, and Poppy said, as she flew to me, "Oh, Mama, your stomach's flat again," and then she met her brother, and he became, for that month he was home with us, the supreme pleasure of her life, and the two of them of ours.

Toto was a big strong fellow, over nine pounds at birth. He could hold up his head and follow a moving finger with his eyes before he was a week old, and he had a grip of iron. Nevertheless, he put on no weight, and he breathed with a rapid shallow movement of his ribcage. Poppy hadn't breathed like that. But the pediatrician said babies often breathed that way, and to supplement his feeding with formula. He developed a rattling cough, and an odd look of doubt or flickering anxiety more and more often disturbed the characteristic marvelous benignity of his small countenance. But the pediatrician couldn't hear anything in his chest, couldn't even hear the heart murmur now, and said to supplement his milk with cereal. He was less alert now in his fifth week of life, and sometimes his eyes rolled strangely and his head fell back as if he were fainting. A second opinion diagnosed heart failure arising from a suspected double heart defect.

They ran a catheter into his heart and found what they suspected. When we visited him that day I looked once and couldn't look again. Eli held him, but he wept so much over the child that the nurses couldn't stand it and asked us to leave. He was operated on the next day, successfully. In the evening they let us see him—a breathing tube down his throat, the respirator beeping, the heart monitor flashing, tubes for blood transfusion and liquid nourishment sprouting from his tiny body—and we saw him as cured. With one hand, I thought, they make genocidal weapons; with the other the means of restoring a dying baby to life. Eli said, "We will celebrate Toto's birthday twice a year—the day he was born, and this day that he was reborn." But less than three weeks later he was dead. "We couldn't save him, the doctors couldn't save him," Poppy kept stating, restating, her small palms stretched out open and upward, while the tears burst from our eyes like hailstones.

He had eyes, and chose me. He loved me for the very reasons that by traditional and prevailing standards disqualified me for wifehood; and thereupon he married me. I had not thought I would marry—not since that day in my twelfth year that our French primer, innocently introducing us to the imperative mood with "Ne vous mariez pas, mes filles," provoked teacher to a sustained vindication of that state of life unto which, inasmuch as it had pleased God to call our mothers, it would please him likewise to call us, and, therefore, naturally, please us to be called. All of us but one. "Non!" said the one. "Pas moi! Jamais!" I must have been waiting—I can't tell for how long—listening for somebody to pronounce what I could not myself pronounce; which is not to say that that somebody simultaneously identified and unyoked for me the harness in which I had thus far gone blinkered and hobbled, obedient and unawares, nor that in that moment my eyes were opened and I knew that, notwithstanding my gender, the wide world was mine from that day forth. I have had my epiphanies, and that was not one of them. Still, I heard the fiat for the deliverance of my imagination of myself in those timely words; so I adopted them forthwith and made them mine.

My mother says I talked myself in. I say it was in the cards long before I could talk. Four sons, so the story goes, was the order my father had put in initially. When his fourth daughter was born he is reported to have fainted in the telephone booth. I was the second disappointment, second in line in the second class. A hearty, cheerful child, I did not at first jib at my station in life: I was bent on excelling in it. If I could not compete in virtue with my elder sister, I could in competence. I was a little mother to my younger sisters; I swept, I dusted, I scrubbed, I sewed: my darning was such, by my mother's nostalgic account, as to be indistinguishable from the fabric it repaired. It was reading, my mother says, that ruined me. But in those days that was a passion subordinated to reason. If, arduously following in my first reading year the fortunes of the little frog who left home to go hopping, go hopping, year after year to go hopping, till he arrived to his astonishment at the very spot he had set off from, I experienced at its stunning conclusion—"The little frog had hopped round the world"—a satisfaction unprecedentedly deep and total; and if, in that same year, the first time I composed a story in writing, I learnt—inky and dizzy with strain—what it was to content my whole soul, it is not to those agencies that I attribute my defection.

The truth is it was my mother herself who ruined me. It was she who described the world for me; inflamed my imagination of it; communicated, like the innocent carrier of an incurable disease, her enchanted vision of this great world of men, which was yet not inaccessible to women of skill and daring enough to assay it. "Charge!" cried Boadicea, and "Courage!" the Maid of Orleans, and "Radium!" Madame Curie. Theirs, theirs, was the glory; mine the homely joys and destiny obscure, which, as it was the express will of God for undifferentiated womankind, was duly the will of my father—the more revered as it was unspoken, the more hymned as it was Mama's exalted function to execute it—for his own undifferentiated four-in-hand. To him we were so much of a muchness that when, once in a while, he saw fit to remark in his awkward, charming way on the conspicuous top-heaviness of my head, I was as gratified as if it were its capacity he had singled me out for, he noticed me so rarely. I was surprised that he knew my name. And all the while, in her indefatigable celebration of his remoteness, his habit of silence, his outrageous indifference to us, as being—no less than his rectitude, benignity, and wisdom—aspects of his sublimity, Mama girded her loins with strength and strengthened her arm. Alas that Father's wages—what with four girls and their dowries to provide for and all—couldn't stand any additional liability, not even a boy, not even the one religious boy among the huddle of Jewish refugee children consigned to our city in 1938. But every Sabbath and holy day that boy spent with us, and every Sabbath eve, came children's bedtime, it was he who got to stay up all hours singing Sabbath canticles with my father. He was younger than Gita, hardly older than me, but Mama said bedtime for girls, and Father said goodnight.

In the happy expectation of war I saw my chance. In the months between the Munich Crisis and the outbreak of war I marched about the streets, accoutred with gas mask and emergency rations, joyfully anticipating evacuation to the country, and freedom heyday, once shot of Mama, heyday freedom.

It didn't fall out that way, for Mama followed us posthaste. It didn't fall out right any way. The forms of Nature, its sounds and smells that have stayed with me from my childhood, are all of Nature in the city. There were never such hollyhocks, pinks, sweet peas, sweet williams in the country, never such scents to inhale into the memory, such wallflowers, roses, wild and cultivated, as made our old backyard gorgeous in the summer. I pined all the war years for our street in the city, the luxuriant Nature there—the horse chestnut at the street's bend that shed its blossom in the gutter, the honey at the base of each petal of the blossom, the life that ran in the water in the gutter; the fruitman's horse, the coalman's, the milkman's; the ecstatic flies gormandizing on the horse's droppings. I pined for the pavement beneath whose black interstices—tread upon them who dare—wolves lurked, bears crouched in ambush: my old stamping ground where I got by heart—from the hooped legs of the factory women, the shaven heads of the children with lice and ringworm, the pallid children running before school to the clinic to breakfast on malt and cod-liver oil, the pallid blackshirts on their Sunday crusades—the grim tale of the urban poverty of prewar England. There were no pavements on the village street to watch from, nothing to watch for; no ragman, no cat thief, no knife-grinder, no lamplighter. There were no lampposts to crouch behind in the dark, soundlessly, sides splitting, one end of a string in hand, the other attached to a neighbor's door knocker. There was no place in the village I wanted to play in, nothing to play at there, no one to play with.

I was on active service in that village—at home and in school and street—all the years of the war. To be Jewish was no crime on our side of the Channel; it was confirmed national policy to save us alive; but that was in flat disregard of village opinion on the matter. There were notes to teacher: "Please don't sit our Doreen next to Jews"; Larry Maffin said Jews wet the bed; they said we killed

Christ; they said the Gerries had the right idea about us. Still, it was less their homespun contumely, as artless as incessant, than the county people's decorous odium that left its indelible mark at the quick. At the party they once gave for all the village children inclusive, there were four guests too many for the big table to accommodate, so whom did they relegate to the overflow table but us four Jewish children, thoughtful in our paper hats.

But it was on the home front that the battle was bitterest. Tyrant, whiplash mother, most deadly of foes because it had been against her back I used to seek consolation in the night; her praise I had striven for, her attention competed for; her zeal, her passions, her tastes that had informed me; her stories, her language, her art that had enchanted me, rejoiced my heart, wrenched my heart; her experience by which I had apprehended the world; the world of her childhood that had been the measure of mine. On Mama's first day at school the handwork assignment was a still life of Miss Fletcher's hat, which Mama so botched that she was dispatched with it to the headmistress, who said, "What a lovely egg cup, Miriam," and gave her a penny. It was that Miss Fletcher who said, when Mama asked in reading class what *rogue* meant, "That's what your father is." But Mrs. Conick laid Miss Fletcher on the stretcher for a similar remark addressed to Ettie Conick about Mr. Conick. The Conicks were the next-door neighbors in Mama's childhood. We knew more about them than about our own neighbors. The Conicks' eldest daughter, Annie, always added, for reasons best known to herself, ten years to her actual age, whereas Mrs. Conick always subtracted ten years from hers, so that a doctor, treating the pair of them together once, was indeed surprised to find among his clientele a mother and daughter of identical age. Annie went blind in later years, from no cause known to medical science. Mama identified the cause right enough though: "Blind from weeping," she said.

"Why did she weep so much, Mama?"

"Alas, poor girl, she never married."

So she could never know the true meaning of happiness. Nobody who isn't married can know it. Mama herself didn't know it until she got married, though she knew plenty else. When Mama was ten she saw her sister Sophie—her mother's darling, the apple of her father's eye—run over by a truck, and die there in the street. "Would to God," said her mother—these were the first words she addressed to Mama at the terrible tidings— "Would to God it had been you!" But Mama couldn't resent that; she understood what her mother felt, because, excepting the boys, Sophie was her best-beloved, and no wonder—such grace, such competence, such wisdom beyond her years. "Which one of us," we asked instantly, "is *your* best-beloved, Mama?"

I thought I had a borderline chance in those days; but that was in the golden age before the war which began that day in September 1939 that Mama arrived with Bebe on her hip, her matchless reserves of rigor mobilized all-out for the task of raising her four little girls, single-handed, in an alien and hostile village, without kosher supplies, in the unremitting observance, nonetheless, of the Mosaic Law— assiduously augmented for the duration with laws of her own making, arbitrarily enacted, daily exercised, with outrageous partiality and bare-faced gall, viz:

"I'm your mother!" tearing open my mail, prying into my journal, despoiling my money box.

"Reading ruins your eyes!" snatching away my life.

"It isn't good for a child to think she's somebody."

"A little snotty-nose I should respect?"

Mama on show in her official capacity, initiating the girls, as becomes a mother of girls, in the art of baking: one measures, two sifts, three pours, four beats—like this, like so, watch me, no talking. Four docile little girls, un-differentiated, undifferentiable, sifting and pouring and whisking and stirring and bowing and scraping in abject servility. Or perspicacious Mama, unscrambling her mess of girls for the edification of an undiscerning public: "That one's the sensitive one, for all her swagger," corroborated willy-nilly by my flaming cheeks and bursting eyes, as I stood there at bay, grinning like a dog.

Self shrinks, shrivels; soul faints with shame. What arms could I bear, in what furnace forge them, against this steamroller, pulverizer, this battering ram, this spirit-breaker, this enslaver of wills, this disgracer of my soul? But who but myself could disgrace my own soul? I was eight: I knew the score. It was not Mama's tyranny, but my capitulation to it; not her terrorization, but my suc-cumbing to terror; not my vulnerability to her copious af-fronts, but the patency of it, my failure to conceal it that disgraced my whole soul.

I devised for myself then a training course in adamantine endurance, inflexible courage, and persevered in it with a rigor exceeding Mama's. I quit the bedroom I shared with my sisters, the bed I shared with Gita, whose sleeping body had been my mainstay against those nightmares in which at my hapless glance all sentient life—dogs in the al-leyway, children at the curb's edge, loiterers at the street corner—writhed, toppled, and guttered out. I installed myself in the little box-room, locked the door behind me, and lay there every night defying the darkness, the as-sassin's breath on my cheek in the thick darkness, and the terrible dreams; defying the air raids, renouncing refuge downstairs lest I fall asleep there and avail Mama of the op-

portunity to pry in upon me and read in my unguarded
face the full measure of her power. I would have lain in
the bilboes to keep my own countenance. But the day the
aeroplane came plunging out of the sky, amputating the
trees, imminently upon us to demolish us before it burst
into flames in the field not three hundred yards from our
house, and I flew, flew, just one of four chicks, instanta-
neously to Mama, involuntarily, uncontrollably, then I
learnt how far short I came of my goal. "Please God," I en-
treated, the instant I knew what I'd done, "don't let her
have noticed," and tore out to the field, swaggering, bois-
terous, shouting down—loud in my clamor to see the
charred bodies—the shame of my uncontrolled terror in
hardly less uncontrolled terror of shame.

I redoubled my efforts then: scourged my flesh to steel
my spirit; stuck pins in my limbs; swallowed—to the
amazement of my sisters—concentrated mustard by the
spoonful without a tremor; suffered excruciating headaches without acknowledging their existence; learnt to
bear Mama's blows, her insults and derision, without visibly flinching; could take to my room on a full day's hunger
strike without capitulating to her battery and assault on the
locked door or to threats of same on my unprovided body.
Crying and kissing in particular I renounced so inexorably
that, long and bitterly as I wept behind my locked door, I
was never seen from my ninth year to shed a tear, though
my sisters watched me, in moments of crisis, like hawks;
and I went also from that time always unkissing and always unkissed. Even Mama—never one to cater to my
preferences—refrained all but one time, which one time I
anticipated with great anguish, praying ceaselessly the entire return journey from a visit to relations duly prolonged
by my succumbing there, shamefully, to measles, "Please
God, don't let her kiss me"; and when God did let her,

"Please God, don't let her tell Gita"; but God let her do that too.

Father, however, could be so unfailingly relied upon to keep his distance that, when he brought the letter that day that determined my future, I took the unprecedented kiss he gave me as his commiserating adieu to all hope for my future. In my time eligibility for higher education was determined by a scholarship examination at the age of ten. Failing that, it was all over for children of our class: at fourteen we would be apprenticed as clerks, shop assistants, factory hands. Gita was in high school already: she wore a uniform; traveled to school by bus with sandwiches in her satchel; studied the liberal arts, the noble sciences. Never in all my life, till Toto fell sick, have I wanted anything more than to win that scholarship. When I did, it was then Father kissed me.

My first day in high school, at my desk, in my uniform, surveying my thirty classmates, all uniformed, all of one age, How gracefully, I thought, they've come through their ten years of life, whereas I, how I've toiled to be ten. I was assailed daily by then by a fugitive voice in my ear at the moment of waking that said I was once homeless, world without end. Exile sat in my chest all morning while I learnt in Physics what a molecule was, and what havoc you wreaked upon untold molecules if you only so much as stroked your desk lid. O world invisible, intangible, unknowable, inapprehensible! But in Maths I learnt what the angle in a semicircle was, and it was that that stood the test at noon when the headaches came, so violently by then as to menace consciousness and plunge me in perpetual shame. But I clutched my desk in the capsizing classroom amid swirling hosts of homeless molecules, reciting for dear life, "My name is Queenie Quesky, and the angle in a semicircle is always a right angle," and by those means did consciousness always prevail.

High school enlarged the scope of my toil, supplied new testing ground for my moral exercise, such as when the overloaded wartime bus, speeding heedlessly past our stop one wintry Friday, obliged us—on account of the imminent Sabbath and the veto against traveling by wheeled vehicle thereon—to take the ten lonely unlighted miles home on foot. There were two roads home—one for me, one for Gita. At the fork I stood fast against her entreaties: "Separate thyself, I pray thee, from me: if thou wilt take the left hand, then I will go to the right; or if thou wilt depart to the right hand, then I will go to the left." How else was I to define myself? Unless I made my way alone, there would be no way at all for me. I remember the look of reproach Gita sent me from those innocent amber eyes of hers as she trudged off on the road she opted for—the longer, lonelier road of the two.

In the summer I took to jumping, to overcome my fear of heights and build up my reserves. I was observed unbeknownst jumping off the quadrangle wall, the storeroom roof, the lavatory roof. My observer and I went swimming together. She looked up at the diving board touching the heavens, then she looked at me. I climbed the steps to the top to go hurtling to my death, to my reinforced life. I was twelve then. I had learnt to swim finally, but I had no speed, no skill of any kind to recommend me then for any race; but I entered for the underwater swimming contest in the annual school sports because staying power was all it required, and I won because staying power was all it required. In the blue woolen bathing suit that had once been Mama's I stayed so long underwater they had to pull me out in the end. I lay on the wet stone, heaving and hawking, ears cocked, eyes on where Mama sat in complacent anonymity in the thick of the hail of astonished applause for this triumph of her handiwork. There she sat, my adversary, the angel I wrestled with all those years of my childhood, to prevail against whom I had scourged my nature, defied the elements, hurled myself through thin air, travailed under thick water, would have walked through fire.

She was my lifeline, my mentor, my best teacher. I have had some marvelous teachers, but none swelled my heart for the great books as she did, who confiscated the very ones she incited me to read, and extolled the passion for them even as she censured it, that mother of mine. It was the very book that had engrossed Mama's reading time the first winter of the war that I lit upon in the city library on our return to the city the last winter of the war. "'Well, Prince, so Genoa and Lucca are to be added to the family estates of the Buonapartes.'" The whole world burst into light for me then. That was an epiphany; and so was the moment, two years later, the eternal moment that poetry, as a phenomenon absolutely distinct from the rhymes and rhythms that had rejoiced my childhood, first made itself known to me:

> *"With what strange utterance did the loud dry wind*
> *Blow through my ear! the sky seemed not a sky*
> *Of earth—and with what motion moved the clouds!"*

These were the voices that told me what I was made for; outrivaled the voice of ageless woe that blighted my wakings; made the world in my heart so huge my heart couldn't contain it. I took to traveling then, schooldays, holidays, regardless: I had an enlightened headmaster. That spring I went up to the Lake Country for Wordsworth's birthday; in the early summer to Stratford-on-Avon for the opening of the annual Shakespeare Festival. I got home that time to find, though in mid-week, the dinner table in festive array and the candles lit. I had forgotten the Festi-

val of First Fruits in the Hebrew calendar, the Feast of
Weeks called Shavuos. Father came in from the synagogue:
"Wordsworth's anniversary," he said, "you remember.
Shakespeare's anniversary you remember. Shavuos you
don't remember." The poets identified me even to my
father.

So I marked out my way early, and it was the world's
broad highway which a young man sets out upon with the
world's blessing, and invested with the imagery of the
great tradition, however otherwise unprovided his way.
Not so the submerged half: we start out to a chorus of cat-
calls from the sidelines. But that couldn't stop my gallop.
Nor could all their efforts to trivialize and deactivate me by
pitting my gender against my spirit withstand the twin
forces—thanks for both to my mother, though far be it
from her to take credit for either—of my long training in
active resistance and the compulsion in me to inherit that
world where such great business awaited me—as wisdom
and understanding to get, laurels to win; revolutions to
bear arms in, garlands to be crowned with; works of art to
adore, works of art to create—that the precipitate engross-
ment of my friends at puberty with clothes and boys and
kissing games at parties struck me merely with uncomprehending astonishment. I did fall in love though, sporadically, in adolescence, first with a young rabbi. But
when I pictured us married, promenading together on the
Sabbath day, greeting similar couples of the Faith, forthwith desire failed, preempted by an imagination of what I
was made for such that no image of conjugal bliss could
rival. It was enough for me that the man at whose feet I sat
spellbound all my senior school years conferred upon me
the chief mark of his favor. It was at my desk he stopped
in his peripatetic discourse, my head he wreathed in the
sleeve of his gown and supported his honored elbow upon,

while promulgating, illuminating, and extolling those books that contain and nourish all the world. I was well satisfied.

But Mama wasn't satisfied. Mama couldn't countenance the way I was going, and neither could anyone else's mama: all out to get me, as shortly appeared, with haute couture and cosmetics aforethought. Off with my decent, noncommittal school uniform; on with the motley, the corrugated coiffures, venal kiss-curls, the stiletto heels, hobble skirt, dress demure, dress décolleté; on with the rig that prohibits movement, precludes feats of heroism, banishes seriousness, all in the one indefeasible cause of sexual allure. But I couldn't say that then, hard-pressed as I was to explain myself. I was far from indifferent to my appearance; but I wanted to look like a girl bound for greatness. The clothes in the shops were for girls bound for doom. I said I didn't want to look like that. "What *do* you want to look like?" Mama asked beguilingly. "Joan of Arc?" Why should I lie to her? "Woe is me!" she resorted for keening purposes to the old tongue. "In a suit of armor fain would she perambulate!" Fain would I indeed, but made do, in the event, with a voluminous raincoat which effectively concealed all my vulnerable body, and which, consequently, I divested myself of so rarely that uninitiated guests in our house took me for a visitor there. Thus appareled I passed the flower of my youth, and thus I set forth, first from home, then from native land, upon my enterprise. "Go," said Mama, when she knew I must, "and gesundheid." Father appeared not to register my going, but when I got to Southampton to board ship he was there on the quayside.

I went out into the world with a heart inside the raincoat pledged to endure, and a face above it testifying to that. The world took me on accordingly; it encountered me all the way without respite. Thus, by the time I met Eli, ten years later, I showed such battered aspect and implacable mien as amply confirmed Mama's grim prognostication of old, when, frog-marching me out of a backyard brawl, into the house, right up to the glass, she had bidden me behold and despair: "What man in his senses, what man not a madman, or gunman, or apeman, would wish for a wife with the face of a *pugilist*?" Eli took kindly enough to it though. He said no Spring, no Summer had such grace as he had seen in my unvanquished face.

CHAPTER
Three

I thought there was no adversity we could not jointly withstand, no enemy that could prevail against the two of us together. I thought that force that moves the sun and other stars, uniting us, made us invincible. But I wasn't persuaded of that in a hurry. The consolidated wind of Israel at Jericho was not more prostrating, I thought, in our inauspicious early acquaintance as occupants of adjoining offices, than his voice through the wall, his demented voice in full blast on the telephone to God knows what earless respondent; his outraged, distraught, despairing, forlorn voice:

> *"Who, if I cried, would hear me among the angelic orders?"*

He was said to be a hunted man: loan sharks, landlords, storekeepers dogged him, brought suit against him, attached his salary; the telephone company ostracized him, the electric company blacklisted him; he lighted his darkness with naked candles, boiled his billy on a spirit-stove; made his apartment a safety hazard; didn't have an apartment.

But at our place of work they provided against such exigencies. While, admittedly, no university in New York City could underbid ours in the matter of salaries, what ours didn't stint on—a bonus they sang still more rapturously the further our wages lagged behind—was office accommodation. It was a pleasure for those of us free to hang out there, like me, like Flaks, with no one at the working day's end to go home to; though Flaks's freedom was compromised, what with Audrey's hysteria and Elinor's sulks—you know what Siamese are—if he didn't get home on the stroke of eight. But for those of us with no home to go to, it was home itself—for Eli Ansell, namely, of whom Flaks said, "He is a man at the end of his rope."

There was nobody Flaks wouldn't hobnob with, no colleague he wasn't on visiting terms with; from the least exceptional to the most exceptionable, he took their soundings, appraised their lives. "His private life, his professional life, Ansell's life every way," Flaks said, "is to pieces. He is shacked up here not to avert his creditors; it isn't even his landlord's doing: his ex-girlfriend won't budge, that's the fact of the matter, and Ansell isn't the man to budge her. Indeed, nothing could induce him to try. He is only too thankful to have escaped with his life. She has slimmed him, he alleges, so relentlessly that his arms and legs are no thicker than pretzels. But he's learnt his lesson, paid the price. That's the last passing affair for him. Not that he has it in mind to get married. He lives only to finish his dissertation. Thirty-three, practically your age, and nothing to show for it—no doctorate, no job security, not a penny to bless himself with, nothing but debts to call his own. He has to shape up fast, get into line, change his life. It's now or never." Exit Flaks, homeward bound to Audrey and Elinor; enter Ansell, if he might make so bold, bearing gifts—a slice of pudding in one hand, a piña colada in the other—to sustain me through the long evening hours. He himself was at work so late on account of his thesis, long overdue; but what could I be working on, he wondered, so late every night of the week? I was writing letters. Admonitory, hortatory letters rolled off my pen by the dozen. Far be it from me, in my capacity as self-appointed keeper of the bourgeois 'conscience, to let slip any opportunity to expose the system by way of the inter-university mail.

To the University Trustees' Ombudsman to Faculty:
Thank you for your invitation to a party in the Faculty Lounge to meet our new Chancellor, which I must decline, since the interests represented by the Chancellor and the interests with which I identify myself are irreconcilable. The Chancellor is hired by our Trustees to manage the University for them. The University is one of the companies they direct. I am enclosing a list of the others, together with their respective capital investment areas and the gross sums invested in them. It is from directors of companies whose capital interests—safeguarded by aircraft and military equipment supplied by the United States—lie in white supremacist South Africa, among other rich fields, that the Chancellor has his appointment. His business as such is to oversee the alignment of higher education with company interests. Mine is to counteract that.

To the Dean of Faculty:
The burden of my letter to you was the economic distress of our graduate assistants. The burden of your reply takes no account of that. I am sorry that your vision is, as you freely admit, subject to your particular temperament; but such an admission scarcely encourages me to take seriously either your view of my polemics as "sophomoric" or

your conclusion that because you see no evidence of the "management-vs.-labor syndrome" the evidence does not therefore exist.

To the Student Committee to End Racism in the United States:

Implicit in your request to all members of Faculty to cancel their classes for two days next week to enable students to attend your "workshops on the larger issues of racism in the United States" is the assumption that mindfulness of such larger issues has nothing to do with formal education. Since I hold no brief for this view, I will not comply with your request. I have already made clear to my students the significance of your marked preference for denouncing racism in the United States as if it were a discrete social phenomenon. Your ostensible solicitude for the victims of racism will doubtless be welcomed by the black bourgeoisie, whose interests, like yours, are vested in the economic status quo. But for the mass of the blacks of this country, as for the rest of the Free World where racism is so freely tolerated and promoted, economic oppression is what racism means. This is what we will be discussing in my classes those two days next week.

To the University Committee to End the War in Vietnam:

I must decline your kind invitation to become a member of your committee, because I cannot identify myself with so significantly limited an aim as yours. The war in Vietnam differs from other wars engineered by United States intervention only in that this one is harder to win. It is harder to roust the Vietnamese Liberation Front, harder to hang out the United States imperialist banner in Vietnam: hence the draft and associated impediments to your wonted middle-class interests. That is why you feel unusually threatened by this war. I am opposed to such a committee as yours, which, in confining its aims to the cessation of only today's imperialist war, and in limiting its awareness to only "the terrible immediacy of the war and its effects on our lives," takes no thought of the morrow's imperialist wars nor of the lives of future generations, here and everywhere.

Yours in the assembly of the hypocrites, Q. Quesky— seen in broad daylight shuffling along the White House circuit, the U.N. Parade, the Pentagon's embattled ha-ha, in rueful misalliance with the interdenominational comrades—assiduously marketing sectarian literature under police safe-conduct—and the multitude enlisted under voodoo auspices, entreating, sometime with lunatic bans, sometime with prayers, the notional mercy of the establishment executive. "Per me si va tra la perduta gente." But where else can I go, and what have I to guide me, now that I have abandoned the self of my old cause-elect to salvage that other self my cause had excluded?

The self that the cause of the oppressed excluded? Fleshpot self? Mess-of-pottage self?

Heart-of-hearts' self that the dogma excluded, cogitative self whose lifeblood is freedom.

While the people perish.

"Myself when young," I said to Ansell, "aspired to the heroic life; but though that was not all I set my heart on, when the time came for me to appraise my priorities, there were no two ways about it. Other gratifications I could forgo at a pinch, but glory and honor I had to have. Fat chance England offered for that; fat chance Europe, ever since peace broke out in Spain. So I set my course for South Africa. That was ten years ago. I had a terrible time there. I got no satisfaction, no glory, no honor."

"What did you get though?"

"I got a political education. Unsupplied as I was in other respects, with that aqua vitae my cup brimmed over—which had its commensurate after-effects; but those, predictable as they were, couldn't have borne advance contemplation. I was so tied to England: all those grim years it was home thoughts of England that had upheld me, as if England were the Beloved Republic that feeds upon freedom. But when I did at last get back to England, for all that I'd been so homesick for it, it wasn't home any more. I was frantic at that. I wanted my warm old niche back again; but the warm old illusions that rested in—South Africa had done for them. I couldn't get over it. I didn't know what to do with myself there. Not that I know what to do with myself here. I write these letters all night, exposing, denouncing, prophesying ruin."

"May one ask at whom you level your prophecies? Ah," he sighed as I told him, "I daresay you don't find your addresses to them a worthy application of your political experience. Objective conditions are not such here, alas, as to induce that lot to take you seriously. They won't; but there's a Marxist group uptown I know of that would."

"No," I said, "I'm not taking up with the comrades again. Fatuous as it is to campaign on my own, I can't stand shoulder-to-shoulder again. That's no reflection on my old comrades. It's my failure, not theirs. I know what I owe them. Not to disparage your uptown Marxists, wherever they got their political schooling, but I got mine straight from the horse's mouth—veteran horse, peerless mouth. They enlightened me with a vengeance, those comrades. I got more than I bargained for, so much more that I can't ever again belong where I used to. But I can't belong with the comrades either, hard as I made believe that I could, which took some doing. 'The reactionary

Dostoevski,' they said, 'the notorious Plato.' 'Still, we can't do without them,' I argued at first. 'Who is we?' they said. That was all they need say. Who was I—an ignorant, privileged stranger—that they should trust me, include me, give me a part to play? In this world you don't get anything for nothing. 'The reactionary Dostoevski,' I snuffled, 'the notorious Plato.' Masters, what lack I yet? Undivided affections. Of all the comrades to fall in love with, which one should I pick on—each to its own kind —but a chronic backslider of Liberal proclivity. We had plenty of them, mostly equally culpable; but some of them were expelled, some of them weren't, according to the predilections of the leadership. I could have winked at that—overscrupulosity isn't one of my failings—but winking wasn't enough in this case. I was required to affirm it, stand up and be counted."

"And you did that?"

"And I did that."

"So he was expelled?"

"Very justly expelled."

"So you parted from him?"

"In public I did. In public I denounced him for dear life; but in private—he was all I had in South Africa—in private I went on consorting with him."

"Did they ever find out?"

"They didn't; but I found myself out. I found I couldn't give precedence to the Cause, when it came to the test; I couldn't abide by what matters most."

"Perhaps that isn't what matters most then, to you."

"What is it that matters most to you?"

He pondered briefly. "Intelligence and sex," he replied, "in that order."

Intelligence and sex, while the people perish. Even so, I observed the saying.

The following night I took him a peach. That was the first time I had set foot in his office. He was shaving. Clothing hung from the walls like pennants, and pages of a manuscript heaped up in sagging drifts about the floor met me in a flurry at the threshold. Retrieving a vagrant page, I remarked that his punctuation certainly was unorthodox: not one full stop in three hundred words. "If there is one thing in that thesis I will never give up," he stiffly replied, "it is those semicolons."

Intelligence, sex, and semicolons. Know your priorities. But I observed that saying too.

"There he goes!" said Flaks. From where we were sitting in the window of the diner, I glimpsed Ansell exiting from the delicatessen, his nightly scoff secured, crossing the road diagonally towards our office building. "He calls you the amazing Q.Q.," Flaks added casually. I had hardly noticed what Ansell looked like till that moment, but from that moment forth I never stopped noticing. There he goes, legs first, each thrown up high with a lordly air, but in opposing directions; trunk to follow, at a reclining angle to legs; head last, rotating on its axis as if on ball bearings. Flaks thought that his face must early in life have been put through a meat grinder. "On a visit to a sausage factory when he was in second grade, spellbound by the goings-on in the trough, he lost his balance and went in headfirst. They caught him by the heels in the nick of time, but not before the grinder had done its work on his face." It must have been a gentle meat grinder though, which had only rammed his chin against his throat, only somewhat flattened his great nose, and furrowed his forehead like a field at sowing time. From under his inverted brows his eyes looked out through heavy spectacles, still bulging, as if in quite recent receipt of the knowledge of how this world goes, but more enlightened than appalled: earnest, medi-

tative, guileless. His thick graying curly black hair shed its
luxuriant seed at random, growing with gusto, as well as
wherever hair commonly grows on a man, in his ears, on
his throat, the skin of his nose, his fingers. There was
no accounting for his physique but as an experiment, the
limbs tacked on to the trunk provisionally to test for effect,
serviceability regardless—the effect being such as to arouse
concern in the beholder, invite question, conjecture. For
how long could that trunk be held up by those legs? What
muse inspired those fancy arms that could bend like pipe
cleaners this way or that, each thumb curling back to the
wrist in full circle? Did his Maker smile his work to see?
Outmatching the sum of those grotesque parts, the whole
was so nearly aesthetic, so touching.

He called me the amazing Q.Q. I pursued our acquaintance, applied myself forthwith to reading *The Interplay of*
Time and Character in Shakespeare: Comic and Tragic Dimen-
sions—his dissertation-in-progress; then, seeing how much
there was in him to know, I offered him house room till
the summer, when, his dissertation completed to the last
semicolon, he would be off to Europe, to England, where
Xanthe resided, his heart's darling. In his wallet he carried
an antique snapshot of her at the age of two. I studied
the wistful little blob standing all on her own in her crib.
"What does she look like now?"

"She has a great, an original face," he sighed, "she looks
like no one else on this earth."

"If you had only two years left to live, how would you
live them?"

"I'd go to Xanthe," he said from his heart, "and make
her take me in."

May her house, in that event, be founded upon a rock!
When he moved about indoors the furniture followed him:
fixtures, at his approach, skipped like rams; movables like

little lambs. Upholstery took upon itself, like St. Veronica's handkerchief, his indelible imprint; paintings deserted the walls they hung on to cling luxuriously to his back. Substance melted in his presence, as of its own accord, into accidence; and so would I have done too, had he given a sign.

As it was, I mended his torn pants, bandaged his torn knees; but if I scoffed in the slightest when he made moan, "Your sanctimony is less than amusing," he said. I ironed his shirts. "You call this ironed?" he said. I made him puddings. I took out a bank loan for him; then another. I ran hither and thither procuring replenishments of the prescription medications indispensable to him at that time of crisis. I bought him a toothbrush. I proofread his thesis; revised awkward passages; solicited his applause for my revisions. "I don't want you monkeying with the *meaning*," he said. A spoilt boy; but that was the worst of him. He told me no lies. He talked to me, listened to me, shared with me, let me help him, took notice of me, didn't begrudge me his time, though he was working round the clock, still typing his last chapter at the moment of departure. He embraced me tenderly then, in one hand his typewriter thumping my coccyx, in the other a five-pound bag of sugar he had snatched up distractedly, its contents sibilantly adrift down my back.

I had a bad summer, what with the ants; a loneliness not sharp but deep; and—in a toilsome attempt to restore the living-room door, unhinged by Eli's exits and entrances— an unsightly injury to my feet, which so grossly altered their shape and size that, when our head of department abruptly summoned me to an audience, I was obliged to go shod in Eli's galoshes. I shuffled across the square to school, expecting a well-deserved promotion, and not unreasonably either, for though admittedly he hadn't breathed the word in the past year, he'd breathed it often enough in the first flush of our acquaintance, reaffirming his faith in his own intuition and daring in picking me off the streets, so to speak, and hiring me at a venture when I had dropped in there, two summers before, on the chance of a job. However, the word he was breathing now was dismissal, with one year's notice.

"But you said," I gasped.

"Did I put it in writing?" he countered incredibly. "When I asked you last fall about your plans for the future, when I asked how you saw yourself five years hence, 'Into battle,' you said—I'm quoting verbatim—'Into battle, standards flying, swinging the old scimitar,' you said."

"Did I put it in writing?"

"You've put more than enough in writing," he came out with it, adding basely, "payroll makes no provision for swinging scimitars here," as I made my exit, its dignity moderated by the galoshes.

I made a long detour home by way of the Indian Embassy, thinking, once in India, to join the untouchables— no more fitting a consummation of my life having suggested itself to me since retiring from the Revolution. But it was after hours by the time I reached the Embassy. Sore-footed, unaccountably sore-hearted, from my ringside seat backing the park I regarded the city, great junk heap of the Western world, which inch by grudging inch I had come to be so much at home in. In the late afternoon, in the late summer heat, it was vile, its untouchables in dribs and drabs stopping by ever and anon with their routine appeals, which so far I had never acceded to without bethinking myself of Marx: "Charity degrades him who gives more than him who takes: treads the downtrodden still deeper in the dust; demands that the pariah shall first beg for mercy before your mercy deigns to press—in the shape of an alms—the brand of degradation upon his brow." But now, listlessly waiving the issue with Marx, I degraded myself, pressed the brand of degradation upon brow after brow.

Back at my place again, minded to wash everything, down in the dim, waterlogged basement where the sorry leftovers of an obsolete rock group and a quartet of deaf-mutes kept improbable company, I'd as lief have thrown myself into the machines with the washing, thrown the whole basement in, the whole city in. A fluid thicker than water was filling up the galoshes. I paddled to the elevator, which came down with a rush. As the door slid open a de-lighted roar burst upon me like applause. I had forgotten how tall he was. How fresh and charged he looked, how inexplicably anciently familiar, how dear to me. How kindly he watched, as we entered the apartment, while I dredged my feet up from their dank coops. They came out bloodily, with a sucking noise. He screamed and fell about most gratifyingly. It was like a salve; and thus solaced I made bold to ask how he'd fared with Xanthe. "More peaceably," he replied at once, "than ever before, now that she knows beyond reasonable doubt what she's always sus-pected me of in her heart. I'm not for her. I'll never make the big time."

"But is that what you want, to make the big time?"

"What I want," he said, "is the guarantee of a job in my chosen profession."

"I've been fired," I announced then, "I'm going to India."

He made no protest; but even though his own apart-ment was rid of its erstwhile incumbent by then, he'd brought his traps to my place, was already cramming his stuff into the couple of drawers in reserve for him still from the last time round. The next month it was the whole chest of drawers; and the month after that he gave up his own place permanently, and moved into mine with all his effects, *inter alia* one brass bed with mattress. "We are well matched," he said as we lay in it, "there is trust between us."

Though at first I reminded him regularly that in less than a year I was bound for Calcutta, my reminders evoked no exhortation to stay, not even so much as a sigh of regret. "I have to commit myself," I volunteered disingenuously. But he was hardly less preoccupied now that his dissertation was done with than when he was still in its throes. "Woe that too late repents for having squandered away the best part of ten years," he groaned. What with the job market in his beloved field shrunk to a shotten herring, and his being no closer to tenure than when he was fresh out of graduate school, he was in a sweat now about job security, about having a job the year after next, and the year after that, and the year after that. One thing for sure he was not sweating about was my not being there in those years ahead. So I settled for that, I was so happy with him to talk to, to listen to, who was so articulate, sentient, discerning; who could always, however galled or galling, be appealed to; who folded up in bed in such a way; who was such a pleasure to behold, to embrace. I used to clutch his hand, his arm, blindly, involuntarily, in the street, in broad daylight. What was I doing? That wasn't my way. I'd unhand him abruptly, but he'd hold it fast, "You are all right, Q.Q." So holding his hand became my way, as did many a way I had not known was mine.

He brought none of the ossifying procedures, ancient or modern, prescribed for relations between men and women to bear on me. He held no brief for the specialization of labor according to anything but ability; so I could cook little messes for him freely. I could mend his clothes without playing myself false, because he would never have me be-

lieve that certain chores were a function axiomatically
of my gender, like the fellow, for instance, on the boat
to South Africa, who had said, when I unceremoniously
tossed back the shirt he had tossed me for mending, "Well,
you're a woman, aren't you?" which a passing pickthank
promptly cashed in on, falling over herself—"Give it
here," she said—in her lickspittle zeal to pay her lickspittle
devoirs. Neither—on the other side of the same coin—
would Eli ever think to impute to me, as my onetime true
love in South Africa did with unctuous intent, the mind of
a man or the heart of a man. He never sought to split off
my gender from me, my visible shape from what animated
it. So the old rift the world had made in me between the
visible and the invisible self began to close up. I no longer
beheld, when I looked in the glass, imminent divorce between body and soul; I was less prone than I had been to
walk into mirrors, more apt to recognize my reflection in
the gesticulating figure in my path, because he said to me,
"You are all right, Q.Q. There is considerable trust between us," and to Flaks he said, "She is the joy of my life."
    He was awarded his doctorate, and he was reappointed,
but at the same rank—the lowest rank—and with no
salary increment. "This is an insult," he said, and com-
menced seeking near and far for a job in his field at a rank
and salary that was not an insult. Near there was no such
job; far, in the Californian backlands, there was such a job.
He came in with the letter of appointment just as I was on
my way out at the double to the dentist with a root-canal
that was blowing my head off. "God forbid I should stand
the hazard alone. We had better get married at once," he
said. So it was given me to experience the soul's bliss that
day simultaneously with the body's torture, as I sat in the
dentist's chair, my heart singing hymns at heaven's gate,
while the sweat of agony streamed down like tears.

I restrained my heart from singing aloud though, loath as I was to sanction the glee of those seeing in my eleventh-hour surrender their pieties vindicated, pride licking the dust. But if I broke my news gruffly to my public at large, to my family I broke it with the most assiduous phlegm. For in all Mama's arsenal of effects for scoring me off in my battle-scarred youth, none had so unerringly hit the spot as her repeated avowal that one of these days I would come home to find a bridegroom from bridegroom-land (handpicked by her on Father's say-so) whom, sure as fate, I would instantly fall so madly in love with that there and then—so much for my high-flown idea of myself!—down on my knees, I would pray heaven fasting he should only make me his wife.

But though the long years of my spinsterhood since then had quite worn out Mama's presumption, her hope remained no less lively for that. None of us Quesky girls married young; but Gita had made it before she turned thirty, thus rolling—as our aunt Frady put it—one great stone off our mother's heart. Then Surrie made shift to roll off another. "Thank God, Miriam," said Frady on that occasion, "now you've only got Bebe to get off your hands."

"And Queenie," Mama reminded her dauntlessly.

"Queenie!" Frady scoffed. "Don't aggravate yourself, Miriam." Her legs gave way under her at my glad tidings; but no response of my kin's was less than dramatic: Gita passed out cold, Surrie had hysterics, Mama and Bebe pulled themselves together sufficiently to inform Father that evening while he was hymning the Sabbath's arrival, chanting its praises and pouring the wine, which he went on pouring and pouring and pouring till it streamed in a hymeneal libation over his hands. Mama called from England, casting up at me how madly in love I must be, but with such utterly dazzling joy in her voice I could hardly find it in myself to gainsay her.

From Eli too I took care to conceal my full heart, though for quite other reasons: for fear of its being a burden to him: I was getting so much the best of the bargain. Not that I didn't have to pay my scot. My beloved, my never-failing heroic imagination of myself had to go, pensioned off, out to grass. Farewell, my lodestars, Joan of Arc, Antigone, unhusbanded Cleopatra. But the parting was timely; I didn't begrudge it. With Eli for my companion I could outface any catastrophe, be happy with him if we lived on Skid Row. But he didn't have equal luck in the draw, he left me in no doubt about that. On our way to the pawnshop to buy the ring he fell to calculating aloud how best to apportion his time in the year ahead—the teaching days of the week in the boondocks with me; the rest with old friends in his old alma mater, some eighty miles from Meridian, our prospective abode. I felt chilled to the bone in the sparkling June weather; my throat, horrifyingly, filled up with rocks. But why should that hurt me? Why should he spend the whole week with me, or tote me along wherever he went? Wasn't he doing enough for me? Wasn't half the week gift enough for me? Still I daren't raise my head, daren't utter one word. "It was only an idea," he laughed tenderly, massaging my head with his big warm paw, "don't take it to heart."

We were married in a synagogue and according to ortho-dox ritual, for our parents' sake. Eli crushed the wine glass underfoot, on purpose for once, and kissed me under the canopy. And with that I became his wife.

CHAPTER
Four

A marriage of true minds indisputably though ours was, it was a strain for me seeing myself as a wife, no disputing that either. The ranks of wifehood yielded no precedent suiting my purposes, no guiding star lighted my married way. Yet I didn't, albeit unexemplared, go undefended. I believed with a passion—as if that in itself were my best defense—that Eli stood daggers-drawn against the rule-book's prescription for wedded wives, that in our relation to one another he and I owed nothing to the copybook roles. Thus, when, scarcely a week after we were married, in company, for the whole world to hear, he ordered me thunderously to shut up, I knew, even as I shut up in mid-word—the graven image of a wife made tongue-tied by authority—I knew this could not possibly be what he wanted. And sure enough, before I could get to the door he was there, intercepting my covert getaway with a quick penitent hug. But it wasn't for him to be penitent—I'd got it all figured out already—I had it coming to me, his rebuke, with my unremitting gala recitals, of Wallace Stevens this time. And what, pray, was the sum of my knowledge of Stevens? Half a dozen poems—five, now that I counted—but only breathe his name in my presence to have me at concert pitch: hear him; hear me—puffed-up poseur, overdue for deflating, all the better for it, much obliged to Eli, he'd done me a favor. Still my heart bled as if flayed. Go reason with that. Couldn't he even tell me to shut up?

Let him tell me in private then. Why all of a sudden so zealous to make it a public issue? And since when had they been such a thorn in his flesh, my party manners, anyway, as to warrant a proclamation to that effect? Hadn't he, only a brief week ago, knowingly, purposely, married a talker, and a clubbable one too? But that, married, precisely, was what had done it—lumping him together with me in the public eye so unreservedly, what recourse did he have but disclaiming against the shame of it? Who can suffer shame gladly? Never mind gladly, no marrying me without suffering it: a package deal, no waivers, no loopholes; no cure for it either: I had it from birth, congenital indecorum, like original sin.

Still, since that didn't constitute the sum total of my worth to him, what ailed him that he was so sedulous these days to have it believed what small beer he thought me? I was never one to be familiar or fond or to kiss before folks: enough for me had he seemed before folks, if not to hold me dear, not to hold me cheap either. But at parties he took to collaring me, in mid-conversation, "We're leaving now." How was I supposed to reply to that? Yes, my lord? No, my lord? You are merry, my lord? How was I to gainsay him in audience all those times he gave the world to believe that the rock our communion was founded on was nothing but sand? How it rankled in me, burrowing in there as if licensed so to do, intent though I was on seeing myself as above all that when it came to Eli—magnanimous, without rancor, unself-concerned.

Thus plying between the two of them, busy being mag-

nanimous here, busy rankling there, there wasn't an idle
moment for me that first year we were married, the year
we spent in Meridian, though uneventfully on the face of
it. For me the outstanding event of the year was our visit—
my first—to Eli's parents in Los Angeles, no more than a
day's drive for us now, hell-for-leather down the motor-
way. The first moment I clapped eyes on them I knew I
was home free. His mother flew to the gate to meet us,
exactly as I'd expected; his father, replying to Eli's how-
are-you, "It's getting nearer," and naming it, "Eternity,"
with that deep inward smile—I would have known him
anywhere. They were both exactly as I'd expected; no
strangers to me; I'd done my homework, getting from
Eli's complex data—here a little and there a little, sorting
wheat from chaff—the very picture I'd wanted to get: parents of much the same background as mine, possessed of
much the same values, just as sure to be predisposed in my
favor as mine were in Eli's. I reckoned they'd be delighted
with me.

Alas, I reckoned without my hosts. Let alone delighted,
they took so little interest, as shortly appeared, in me and
mine that, for all my daily unflagging labors to make myself known to them, I felt on the last of the ten days we
spent with them more surely a stranger than on the first
when his father, astonishingly, had asked if I worked in the
Civil Service; his mother wondered if I were still of child-
bearing age, why I didn't wear lipstick, if I had enough
aprons. Aprons? For the housework. Housework? "As
long as you take good care of Eli," she conceded in parting, "that's all that matters," which prompted me, soldier-
ing on to the end with the job of identifying myself to her,
to an earnest discourse on those loftier considerations at
work in my marrying that man and his marrying me.
"You call him a man?" his father snorted. A man com-

pletes his dissertation on time; a man wears a suit, owns a
house, has money in the bank, insurance policies; a man
has a tenured job.

"My first publication," Eli announced incautiously,
wishfully making his father a present of it.

"And your last," said his father.

Not, observably, the most gracious of fathers; nor, when
I came to think of it, suppose one had something to write
home about, the most receptive of fathers to write home
to. But I didn't come to think of it then, nor for ages after,
it so rankled in me that Eli, nothing loath, had brought me
into their fastness without having taken the requisite measures to pave my way, without even having troubled to tell
them we'd met as colleagues. My Jewishness, that was his
sole disclosure, which, admittedly, did satisfy their bedrock requirement; yet just where their business with me
began, just there, evidently, it ended, as if in their son's un-
forthcomingness they had read their cue for indifference.

But I wasn't one to settle for that: nothing daunted, I set
to with a will to woo them, make myself one of them,
stimulate their interest wherever I could find it. So when
they asked in their listless way if I had any family in America, I came in at full bat. Indeed I had family in America,
and, as good luck would have it, for I hadn't yet met him,
living practically within spitting distance of them—my
uncle Noah, the only one of my father's kin to survive the
war. How he'd done that was no everyday story; but I
didn't hesitate then and there to relate a chapter; nor did I
omit to apprise them of our appointment with this same
uncle of mine the following day.

We kept the appointment in his scruffy, downtown Los
Angeles backyard, in the shade of a sizable brick outhouse
he had just put the finishing touches to, which he said he
had waited for twenty-three years, from the day he left

Dachau on a stretcher till the day he retired, to build, with
his own hands exclusively, to the memory of Lithuanian
Jewry exclusively. I didn't give him my argument against
exclusivity, he was hard of hearing, anyway—deafened in
one ear by a blow from a guard at Dachau—so it took him
all his time to hear what he did want to hear, let alone what
he didn't. The Yiddish press had called it a holy place.
Twin cenotaphs to Kovno and Vilna overlay all its interior
floor space; and on the wall at their head REMEMBER RE-
VENGE was writ large in Hebrew and English, underlined
by a frieze of photographs of his countrymen in extremis.
The Yiddish press had urged him to make it a public be-
quest. To whom else, being childless, was he to bequeath
it? I suppressed with an effort an unaccountable impulse to
urge him to leave it to me. Suppose he did, what would I
do with it?

We got back half an hour late for dinner. Eli's mother
was bristling: "Couldn't you have told whoever it was
we serve dinner at six o'clock prompt in this house?" I
couldn't believe it. I stood there at a loss, while Eli said
nothing; just tossed me to them like a piece of flotsam,
anomalous jetsam, without credentials, unhistoried. He
betrayed me to them that day with his silence, and the next
day betrayed me to them with his clamor, calling me pe-
remptorily into the house from where I was recollecting
myself under cover of hanging out the washing at the far
end of the yard. I tore indoors straight to the telephone,
but that wasn't what he'd hauled me in for: a cuisinier on
the color TV was showing the world how to core green
peppers. If we'd been on our own, I would have watched
gladly; once apprised of his partiality for cored green peppers, I would have promptly made shift to learn how to
core them, inasmuch as it was understood to be no more
my conjugal function than his. But here he was now, all

agog to advertise to his parents what manner of married
man he was, what manner of wife he would have me be—
the image of what they would have me be: docility in an
apron, coring green peppers.

Fat lot any such sop to their predilections could do
to jack up his credit with them, anyway. No credit due,
none forthcoming, short of his crushing himself into their
mold, making a down payment on a house of our own, in
Meridian yet—he had a safe job there, every prospect of
tenure, what more did we want?

We wanted New York. We wanted out of that house-and-
garden, faculty-wives-club, two-car-garage funk hole, and
back to New York where we best belonged, the bleakness of
job prospects there notwithstanding. Not that we were
proposing to double back without one job between us to
bless ourselves with, no question of that; but no question
either, that toehold secured, of our stickling for more. As
for Eli's inveterate misgivings about his professional future, that was his father nagging in him; I hadn't married
his father. So when—only because they could pay me less,
seeing I had no doctorate—it turned out to be I, not Eli,
who landed the job enabling us to return to the in-
salubrious city we were so homesick for, let anxiety crease
up his face like a concertina, let him take to munching on
tranquilizers like candy, I only more strenuously exhorted
him to bristle his courage up. And even when, on receipt
of the last of the letters of rejection, he burst, terrifyingly,
into tears, still I couldn't see for the life of me what there
was to be worried about. We had each other; we had one
whole salary between us, and, to subsidize that, a voluntary long-term abundant loan from a well-heeled old
friend; then, on top of that, just as I'd predicted, a job offer
came in for Eli too—a stand-in for the next half-year; and
so we were in all things well. Only his besetting anxiety,

far from lifting now that he'd cast the die, fastened upon him like an incubus, and, impervious, like for like, to my exhortations as I had been to its pleas, accompanied us relentlessly back to New York.

We returned to the beloved city in the early fall; found an apartment, paid the security on it, the agent's fee, the first month's rent; moved in with our brass bed; a baby carriage on long-term loan, due for tenantry come January; and our goods and chattels, such as they were, well sufficing our modest needs. But it took Eli's mind off his misery, buying furniture, so with furniture we bought off his anxiety awhile. We shelled out some five hundred dollars just for a sofa to sit on. The sofa, as far as I was concerned, got the best of the bargain. Heavily as I sat on it, it sat more heavily on me. How, if there were a fire, the thought nagged me obsessively, were we ever to get that sofa down the fire escape?

My school began a week before Eli's. Off I went, belly swinging low, but high-hearted still. We were home again; and what if Humanities departments here, as throughout the land, had altogether ceased from hiring, yet in this city of tricks, devices, starting holes there was somewhere a permanent job for Eli, blackly as he denied it. Only four months to go for our first ewe lamb; then we'd have another; then another; and all live together, come wind, come weather, merrily, merrily. A long way to school, twice changing trains in the barbarous subway, then a bus ride to take. I got lost on the way there, kept getting lost on the sprawling campus, waddling off course the livelong day, and, what with their voluptuous swell, in stockinged feet too ere the sun went down.

I did, in the end, find my way home, but not to find Eli waiting there. Oh, where is my wandering boy tonight? Unconscious on the bathroom floor from an overdose of the tranquilizers he'd grown even more partial to lately than speed. The next night he was on the kitchen floor. But that was that; twice was enough; he'd learnt his lesson. He was as good as new by the day his school started.

He taught late hours, so I always got home well ahead of him, and left in the mornings ahead of him. Undoubtedly, coming home to await the sight of his face as he came through the door—always the same now, adamantly black, bitter, inconsolable—was worse than setting off to the sight of it in the morning. But then again, I couldn't decide. At night, in bed, his face obscured by the kindly darkness, we huddled together: there was always that, his beloved warm ever-friendly bulk to console me. Undoubtedly, the mornings were worse. Off to school, waly waly as often as not now, for him, for myself, because I was powerless to help him: all my will, my bright ideas, my labors to pump him with hope from my own inexhaustible wellspring of hope, all my faith in him, these availed him nothing. So I didn't know why I was going off in the morning, coming home at night, from him, to him, when what use he had for me, if any, baffled my understanding; certainly my being with him seemed to make no difference. Enough of that. He had use for me—though, never lavish with compliments any time, of late he had hardly acknowledged it—he had use for me as much as he had for the air he breathed. He didn't consider the merits of the air he breathed either. And what if I could no longer make out what his marrying me had to do with me in particular, still he hadn't picked me out of a hat to live with for keeps, nor was his lowering and glowering morning and night the whole story either. I was trudging home belatedly from the prenatal clinic one wintry evening, when he lurched into view, coming to find me, and sighting me, smiled suddenly, hugely, with a radiance that lit up the night.

There were moments enough to match that, intermittent, but each of such concentrated grace as over the long haul so sustained me and so permeated my life with him that even when, at Toto's going, the mere grasshopper became a burden, this whole world a capsizing dustbowl, still I knew myself signally favored in having Eli for my companion in it. And, proof against all my subsequent pronunciamentos to the contrary, this knowledge endured.

As if to order, Poppy was built on the grand scale, lying under construction a good month more than full term before she sprang fully armed, as it were, upon the scene where she was to be relied on so heavily. In the forty-fifth week of that pregnancy, Feffer, sick of the sight of me, gave three days' notice of intent to deliver the child by Caesarean section, which, since it was only unnatural births our medical insurance covered, delighted me. But Poppy had it her way after all, dispatching us to the hospital that very night, a snowy one. They sent Eli away, and gave me an enema, then left me alone to die in the bathroom; then they hung me up by my hands and feet from midnight to noon, with nothing to while the time away; nothing to eat, not a nut, not a raisin, for thirteen hours; and no one to talk to, till, "Push!" Feffer began to roar like a drill sergeant in my ear. "Dr. Feffer," I pleaded against the shouting, the impossible pain, the awful monotony, "what about a little civilized conversation for once in a while?" He said, "Push, you kook!" I said I couldn't do two things at once, I was trying not to scream. "Push!" he screamed. Shortly afterwards he said, "You've had a girl, big enough for school already." Then they wheeled me into a cupboard that passed as a ward, where together, Eli and I, respectively overwrought and unshaven, battered and famished, studied our firstborn, and she studied us out of gray eyes wide-set in her huge bald head, pleasantly, with a serene, approving air, as if blessing us. "The next one," said Feffer to Eli, "will drop out." To me he said, "You've had so many stitches, when you screw again it'll be like starting from scratch." He added lightly, "Your bladder's gone into shock, by the way, but not to worry." Not to worry, with Poppy, already grown out of her swaddling clothes, lolling about in the nursery at thirty dollars a day, myself at a hundred a day in the cupboard? "Let me out of this hospital," I said. "You have to pee first," he said. Not till nine hundred and forty dollars later was it given me so to do; but much else was given me in the meantime. So surpassingly had my Eli acquitted himself at his stand-in job that—*pace* his entrenched self-distrust, his pitch-black predictions—his department re-hired him as their Renaissance specialist on a three-year tenure-track appointment, at professorial rank too. And, gift upon gift, from our well-heeled old faithful came not only the price in full of my ransom, but a shiny little motor car too in which Eli rolled up on the day of release to carry us home. Our eternal home, cannonaded straight into Abraham's bosom, I feared, as, westward ho, we plunged into the park, thorough bush, thorough briar, and out again at the other side, and on through the red lights, the no entry signs, the shrieks of the citizenry on foot, the execrations of those awheel.

A grim homecoming we had of it: the place was a shambles: as if vandals had broken in and trashed it, every drawer was pulled out; the refrigerator door swung open; a bookcase had toppled, spewing its contents far and wide; the sofa looked altogether worn out; and the plants were dead. Pills in diverse colors bedizened the floor: blue pills to tranquilize, the yellow to combat their side effects, and the purple ones to combat theirs. The lilac ones, the capsules in silver and pink, and the red and gray reversibles were new to me. He was at it again then. But what was I at, mumpsimus, making mouths, thinking grim this festival day of our jolly Poppy's homecoming?

"A girl," Eli's mother allowed tellingly, "is best, in the long run," while old Father Wormwood himself swelled the telephone wires with his diapasons. Mama stood like a greyhound in the slips, straining upon the start, but I contrived to hold her off for the months I was suckling Poppy, loath, even after all these years, to have my old-time adversary behold me party to an act so tender. As it was, whenever I fed the child in the hospital, at pains to counter its implications, I got myself up like old Nokomis, in miles of beads for the occasion. But once home, with only Eli and Poppy about, no call to address the establishment, no need for my stage props. At first, when I wheeled her out for a breather, it was hugger-mugger, on the ready to whisk us out of the path of any acquaintance espied in the offing. But the shifts my idea of myself was put to with Poppy's birth was a caper compared with its ordeal when I got married. For one thing, even if pregnancy had not already impressively subverted resistance, the margin Poppy allowed for it wasn't wide enough to paw the ground in. She accorded me the identity best sorting with her requirements, tasked me to it relentlessly, rewarded me for it bounteously. In the sixth week of her life, without a moment's notice, she flashed me a smile. They told me the smile came in in the sixth week, but they never said it came in with five dimples. I summoned Eli hotfoot. She gave him her solemn, sincerely approving look. No sooner did he turn his back than she flashed me another, intimate, mirthful, enthralling.

She was never less Eli's baby than mine though: he made that his business from the start, insofar as he was able; and often enough when he wasn't able. In the street, with

Poppy astride his shoulders, he would charge ahead—en avant, à la vie, à la mort—while I brought up the rear, heart in mouth, stifling a scream at every awning, hand clapped to eyes against the imminent spectacle of her blood-boultered skull. But he never, in fact, failed to duck at the awnings, never forgot her huge bald pate above his huge curly one; and though the drugs greatly exacerbated his natural titubancy, he never once fell while carrying her. With her on his back he led a charmed life.

Without her on his back, for that matter, he led a charmed life. It remains to be marveled at how, tempting providence so inordinately, he didn't bring himself to the grave in those years. I myself would not have stickled to heave him into it times in plenty, dating from the night two broken-winded policemen brought him home unconscious, locating his address from the driver's license they found in his wallet, otherwise picked clean, presumably by the glass of fashion who utilized Eli's credit card for one round-trip flight to Miami, one tuxedo, one stetson, one pair of knickers, one cummerbund, and one earring. Offloading their freight without ceremony, the police handed me Eli's smashed eyeglasses; then, marveling disingenuously that his breath didn't smell of liquor, they departed, leaving Eli slumped on the sofa where they'd dumped him, faintly conscious now, his mouth hanging slack, saliva and vomit lacing his chin.

I looked at the cretin he had made of himself: the pervasive, sheer, predominating intelligence that made his face so worthy of study despoiled and shamed; the eloquent, original workmanship of his body trashed; his whole humanness gutted. Rabid, as if it were I he had animalized, I hurled myself at him to tear him to pieces. He fell back helplessly, one arm across his face in a feeble defensive gesture; his eyelids flew up, and, for a moment, I saw in his eyes' depths his anguish. The awful mute pathos of that look and that gesture seemed to split my heart dead center. With one half I panted to finish him off, with the other to solace his unhappy head, rock-a-bye his poor body, make him amends. Nothing Eli ever did made me madder, wrung me as insufferably as that moment, which came unfailingly, every one of those subsequent times I was to fall upon him with murderous intent, to force me to look through the sullied, insensible, vile hulk he made of himself right into the quick of his wasted humanity. As it struck at me, I went at him again with fury renewed, till, fury spent, I could put him to bed.

He was himself again by morning. He never remembered what had gone on in those fits either of his or of mine, never appeared to bear me a grudge for assaulting him. I used to wonder sometimes if all those blows he sustained in his stupor hadn't wounded him beyond consciousness, bruise upon bruise accumulating secretly in the core of his heart. But then again, the ungrudging reception he gave to my fury was for him, perhaps, by way of payment for damages done; even, perhaps, the price of his license to do it again, and again, and again, just as I no less insistently chose, in my own improvident, willful way, to believe his latest attack was his last. Still, however forewarned, what means did I have to forearm myself with?

I could no more accurately predict than he could identify afterwards the immediate cause, what in particular would dispatch him to his medicine chest to consume up to seven times as much as the daily dosage prescribed. In his desperate bid to keep himself going, through tenure, and afterwards, just to keep going, for five years in all, he would bomb out once weekly on average; but sometimes not at all for a fortnight; once not for two months; other times three days in a row. Once he was on the rampage I learnt to lock away pills, confiscate checkbook, wallet, eyeglasses, and car keys; but I couldn't keep him in leading strings. He would leave the house with faculties intact, only returning bereft of them; or the sane enough man I had left at home was run amok by the time I got back. I tried at times, at his request, to keep his drugs under lock and key, doling them out only as prescribed; but he always had his secret caches to draw on, and when they were exhausted he broke the lock. Besides, without his drugs in excess, he could barely move, would lie inert, sometimes sleeping twenty-two hours of the day. The two waking hours he reserved for eating. In those years he ate prodigiously. When he couldn't squeeze into the last of his X-large shirts he went on a diet—that is to say, he added proportionately to his daily fare cottage cheese in enormous quantities to neutralize the effect of the rest.

Without the drugs, or on merely the dosage prescribed, he was torpid; and when he overdosed to the maximum torpid too. But at a certain fine point just short of extreme excess he hummed with activity: up and doing at three in the morning, putting all his affairs in order, and mine, and Poppy's; sorting papers, his and mine; tying them up with miles of string in indisseverable bundles; tying up Poppy's little duds similarly; stowing all securely away in saucepans; turning out drawers; writing checks, from our overdrawn account, for the poor and the maimed and the halt and the blind—his characteristic open-handedness, like all else in him that particularized and graced his nature, traduced and travestied; turning out his pockets, tearing up all the wastepaper, including the paper money, into tiny fragments, deposited in the garbage pail with the garbage, for me to sift through and Scotch-tape together at my convenience. The household reorganized, everything shipshape, ahoy there for Poppy. She was a better sport about it than I was. Then bright and early to school, with his bathing trunks in the dead of winter, unless I got hold of his car keys first. Ad hoc, catch as catch can, these were the only kind of means I had to protect him from himself: measures more radical mostly boiled down to measures unfeasible.

I suppose I could have cut off his drug supplies—his legal ones, that is—at the source: I could have appealed to his doctor; but that would have meant abandoning him altogether to the street dealers. I could have had him committed. I couldn't have done that. I could have had him in a psychiatrist's hands. By Poppy's first birthday he had himself in, which most likely was what held the lid on his brainstorming average, though it wrought no cure. I could have left him, just taken Poppy and left him. Never. Never the slightest question of that. But I was always making as if to leave him, bound in full cry for the telephone directory listings under Lawyers, Divorce. This never failed, however ephemerally, to impress him. He would beg. I was deaf. He would plead. I was deafer. "But we've been getting along," he would wail finally. That was the last straw. Getting along! Even down to such a nadir he would not stickle to plunge us. Cleopatra (she was back again) and her Antony, getting along, like the old gray mare and her stablemate? Had he taken leave of his senses entirely?

CHAPTER
Five

Before summer brought us the first installment of grand-
parents, laden with gifts like packhorses, to pay court to
Poppy, Eli went scouring the neighborhood for a larger
apartment, and found one so spacious, rent-controlled
too—twice the size of our old one for half the rent—that
without a moment's hesitation, fairly clawing each other
for joy, we signed the lease, which, being date-stamped
seven days after the first of the month, gave us a full week's
occupancy rent-free into the bargain. The moving men
came with the van; had Eli check and recheck our new address on the bill of lading; and casting a supercilious eye
upon our chattels to go, said they'd race us there. Get set,
with Poppy in her carriage, go, we took the nine blocks on
foot, and beat them to it; and awaited them there from
noon to dewy eve, and still waited, while, hours ago, at
the very house number, the very street number, but across
the park on the east side of town, in accordance with the
address writ large on the bill of lading, the moving men,
receiving cold welcome, had retired vexatiously to the de-
pot. For unloading at midnight you have to pay double.
For signing the lease of an erstwhile rent-controlled apart-

ment clearly date-stamped a full week after the official decontrolling date you have to pay double too. "With reference to the rent," said the notice they must have mailed to us while our signatures on the lease were still wet, "herein accepted without prejudice to any increase the landlord may be entitled to pursuant to the provisions of the revised control law," and so forth, whereupon we called the landlord, a marvelous witty fellow, who said not to worry, "Doesn't it say without prejudice?" and laughed like a hyena.

In the green of summer came Eli's parents. It augured better for me with them this time, much better. His mother spoke to me now as if she knew something about me; she was trying. "A housewife I don't say you should be, but at home you can also be," she searched for the word, "creative." Eli's father had always provided for them single-handedly; to her mind, what with a child on the scene, it was up to the man, it was Eli's responsibility, to earn the living. "You call him a man?" Eli's father rapped out, but mechanically, engrossed as he was now in wooing Poppy, incessantly hovering over her, enchanted, enchanting. "You want to know how much money I have in the bank for you, my darling?" he was asking her as tenderly as if the size of his savings account were indeed the measure of love.

How the sight of Poppy, appropriately attired for the paddling pool in her sailor suit, made one quite long for the ocean, said Eli, donning his bathing trunks for the occasion. His belly sagged like an avalanche of yeast dough over the waistband. The sight of it made one quite long for oblivion. "Merciful God!" breathed his mother; "a behemoth!" his father. An ominous overplus of jollity in his manner kept me riveted to his side at the pool, mindful that only three inches of water was water enough for a man to drown in. He handed Poppy to me before he sank face-down in it. It took two stalwart men all they had to lever him up again. "He fainted," I said. His parents, most obligingly, at once and in chorus imputed it—antic speech, outlandish gesticulations and all—to his overweight. We lugged him home; and I got him to bed, while they held whispered conference in the living room—putting two and two together, no doubt, I thought wretchedly; and sure enough, "We've been putting two and two together," his mother said, "and here's what we have it add up to: a very strict diet, low-calorie—no bread, no potatoes, no cookies, no exceptions. That's your assignment, it's up to you: for you he'll do it, to us he won't listen; to you he'll listen, for you he'll do it."

If he'd hold the line just while his parents were with us, I wheedled piteously, he could bomb out afterwards, if he liked, for a week scot-free. But came our next family jaunt, to the zoo, his parents, in marked contrast to the great ape, who couldn't take his eyes off Eli—manifestly unable to countenance a repeat performance of any item whatever in Eli's repertoire: viz., sucking his breath for-tissimo, gurgling, snoring, chuckling knowingly, thump-ing his chest, clawing his jaw—headed Poppy's stroller towards the exit, and hived off from us without a word. So the jig was up. The pressure in my thoracic cavity signaled its ultimatum. I was snorting like a horse. If I didn't in-stantly discharge it I would suffocate. My fingernails in the flesh of his arm, I dragged him about-face to the exit to have at him outside, but stopped short at that moment, as shuffling towards us, came such a twosome—a lubberly cretin borne up on the arm of a worn-looking woman—as could surely have passed for our mirror image, except for one thing: Eli's cretinism endured for a day, not a lifetime; and for another thing, the way that woman held that poor fellow's arm and guided his lubberly steps was not my way with Eli, the compassion informing it none of mine. Thus chastened, I loosed my cruel grip on the bruised arm in mine, laid my cheek against it, and held his hand like a friend, at which he bestowed upon me a look of such desperate gratitude from his dull goggles as broke me up altogether. With what cataclysmic sympathy then he fell on my neck a-sobbing! Hands knit, sorrow to sorrow joined, we tottered out of the zoo.

Eli's parents were already home, with Poppy sacked out, by the time we got there. His father said nothing, nor did his mother, until I'd got Eli tucked up, then she said, "He was never like this before." But immediately, sparing me not so much as a moment to gnash my teeth in at this remark, noises off from our bedroom dispatched me thither, to find the bed vacant, to scent him out where he lurked in my closet, his vast bulk stuffed into my best apparel, smoking a joint. Hauling him out, I felled him with one blow. The earth trembled. His parents stood in the doorway. "I hit him," I said, put him back to bed, and rejoined them in the living room, where the glass chandelier was still tinkling from the groundswell. They sat huddled together on the sofa in mute misery. I thought, Their son, their only child; and my heart smote me, till his mother said, "For a wife to hit her husband, that I've never heard of." Instantly I summoned my defenses. "To hit a sick man," she said bitterly, "is that today's fashion?"

Yet it wasn't my trespasses against Eli they were chiefly concerned to deplore, it was his against them. Item, eighteen years ago, leaving home—the first step to ruin—for college; the local college wasn't good enough for his excellency. Item, leaving behind him an overdue library book for his father to pay the fine on. Item, seventeen years ago, home on vacation, damage done to his father's car. Item, that same vacation, cursing father and mother. Item, seven years ago, the price of a movie ticket loaned from an uncle, still owing.

A scandalous record, tut tut, no denying that. But now for the credits. What, nothing of him to approve of, be grateful for? No pleasure in the sagacity, wit, high-mindedness, modesty, gentleness, open-handedness of the son who was all they had, after all, their only child?

And with good reason too their only child, so he should have everything of the best. And fat thanks they'd gotten for it. No pride in his *what*? His achievement? Ten years to get his doctorate. They should only live so long, please God, to see his next achievement. If he'd listened to them twenty years ago, he'd have something to show them they'd call achievement. Where were they, his house, his savings account, his security, his tenure? *He* was worried sick about that? And they weren't worried sick? God knows they were sick, sick at heart at the sight of him, how he looks, a hissing and a reproach, a disgrace to be seen in the street with him.

Appeal dismissed out of hand. Not a chink in their pachydermatous sanctimony to appeal through. And to crown it all, even as I pledged myself for evermore to marmoreal indifference to them and to my failure with them, they frustrated me. "Don't think badly of us, honey," Eli's mother said at their leave-taking. "No hard thoughts," said his father.

In their wake, in high summer, the day Poppy completed her first half-year, came Mama like the water of life to revive us; and Eli and she were fast friends; and Eli kept on the lee side of excess the whole month she was with us, cosseting, cleaning, cooking, reminiscing, while the three of us hung out with her. "It seems so long sometimes since you children were little," she observed, spooning pulped nourishment into Poppy's ever-open mouth, "but other times I wonder, Where have all the years gone?" I knew, without looking, that Eli's eyes must be filling up. She sang to Poppy, songs of her own composition: "Let me squeeze those knees, the squeeziest knees, the pleasiest knees, the unbelieviest knees in all the world." "World," Poppy repeated, clear as a bell. Eli and I shrieked in unison. "Leben!" Mama congratulated her, but without astonishment. "World, she says. How strange it is," she fell to musing, in that voice, with those eyes whose progressive innocence had long since overshot the bounds of propriety, "how beautiful they say it looks from outer space, this world, where there's so much suffering." An insubordinate tear blotted Eli's cheek. "I've noticed," Mama told me tête-à-tête, "that he's very emotional. Be gentler with him. You've got a sharp tongue sometimes." The sort of man, she summed Eli up, so sweet-natured he would run a mile for anyone. How well that augured for Poppy's character! "I knew when I married Father," she told me, woman to woman, "that none of my children would be shallow or mean."

She baked for an army the last week she was with us. "All night long," she reported, passing Poppy a scrap of dough to work on, "I was dreaming of mice." Eli wondered what that could be about. "It's about wanting more grandchildren," she told him shortly. Eli assured her we had every intention. At the moment of her departure, handing Poppy over at last, "I can't tell you," she said, with her radiant, heart-wrenching smile, "what it means to me that you've got Eli and Poppy for your happiness." I protested that I'd been perfectly happy unmarried, unchilded. "With them though, you're more fulfilled." She had to say it, as I had to deny it, hurling my disavowal at her beloved gallant back as she disappeared through the gates. Not since my South African years had I felt such homesickness as I felt then, exiled with her going. It was so acute that every day for weeks afterwards I flew for the mail, seeking the imaginary letter that would make it as imperative as desirable for us to pack bags at once and make tracks for England.

Now, in the sere of summer, while Eli struggled to get his dissertation into publishable shape for the sake of tenure, I sat in the park with Poppy, talking to her about English parks. If I half-closed my eyes, I could make the dry grass look like English grass, catch for a fleeting moment the scent of late wallflowers. "It's so discouraging," Eli said unfailingly every day's end, "discouraging." If the amber summer evening light had been English light, the heavy air English air, the twilight city London city, how tirelessly I could have pumped encouragement into him. These days I couldn't summon the heart in myself to contend with Eli's discouragedness; couldn't find the faith in myself, though in the old days it had coursed through my veins with such force I had believed I could restore life to the dying, just by getting a grip on the wrist recharge the failing pulse from my own dynamo. I had more faith in drugs now. Eli's doctor had changed his prescription. But this new drug worked slowly, slowly; we had to be patient; it might take a month.

Midway in that month, however, I was due back in harness, for which reason we briskly advertised for a weekday custodian for Poppy. The telephone didn't stop ringing for three days:

"Hello, Laurie speaking, qualified baby nurse, have no job now because nearly all babies are born in the spring."

"Hello, are you fine? I am Ella. Have references Mistress Klein, Mistress Newton."

"Hello, I call for a friend who is not speaking English. For that you may pay her less."

From dawn to midnight: "Goodnight, how are you? I call late. Are you resting?"

They gave me something to cry about. Immigrant girls

by the dozen, qualifications, work permits regardless, old women from far-flung borough purlieus came, brightly concealing their desperation, to vie for the job. Gazelle won hands down; and Gazelle, all the while she was scraping together the necessary to get her own little girl out of storage, tended our little girl as devotedly as blithely she accommodated our little girl's father's extravaganzas. His new drug started working the same day as I did, much faster than anticipated, indeed at the double, once the patient, ministering to himself, took to doubling the dosage, as—to judge by the hairy duenna in skirt and shawl ensconced in the kitchen, benignly overseeing a convulsed Gazelle with Poppy gaily astraddle one splitting side— manifestly the patient had. All day long Mr. Ansell had kept her, and Poppy too, in stitches, Gazelle reported, mopping the tears of mirth from her eyes, and falling about reminiscently. And so Mr. Ansell continued to do the two years she was with us.

Those were the frantic years I was running for all I was worth; but still I could never run fast enough to keep up to snuff. We were off on an out-of-town visit. As prearranged, I was to belt home from school, pick up Poppy and the suitcase, and meet Eli at the appointed spot in the railway station. From the subway exit, with barely three minutes to make the train, Poppy on my hip, I floundered through the station, lugging the suitcase, blubbering uncontrollably because I couldn't run fast enough. The train was already vanishing down the track as I reached the platform where Eli was still awaiting us. Not a word of reproach did he utter, but I could have dashed my head in despair against the metal stanchions, because I'd let him down, because I couldn't run fast enough to keep up with the runaway expectations I had of myself. Airborne, how they fled before me!

I couldn't keep up with our creditors' expectations either, more particularly our creditors in the car repair shop and the traffic department. In spring, once the evenings were light enough, just as soon as I was home and Gazelle on her way, Poppy and I would be off on our round of the neighborhood streets in search of the car, which we learnt to distinguish in no time from all other cars of the same make and color by the parking ticket, or two, or three, attached to the windshield. Day after day I should grind at the mill for that car—exclusively Eli's preserve, since I couldn't drive—to sit parked on a yellow line.

"In the long run though," Eli said, "the way train fares are soaring, it'll save us a fortune."

He should excuse my not getting excited about that, what with parking fines on my mind to the sum of fourteen hundred dollars, though, granted, a trifle, compared with—pardon my dragging this up—repair costs.

Shame on me! Was it his fault the car was a lemon?

Day in, day out, I should grunt and sweat to provide for a lemon?

But it wasn't piloting my way through our debts that most tasked my cunning; it was covering for him all the while he sabotaged his prospects for tenure no less relentlessly than he pursued them, so that I was at my wits' end to fabricate more and more elaborate explanations for his irregularities, his absenteeism, his missed appointments, his chronic dereliction of the whole range of duties attaching to a professional work-life. Say, for instance, when he was too bombed out for school, and I'd informed his school office that he was sick, and then the office called back for a word with him, I couldn't keep telling them he was at the doctor's, or fast asleep, heavily sedated; and I couldn't tell them I'd have him call back later, when he was out for the count for the next twelve hours. Yet I always contrived to keep his cover for him at work, never let him down in that respect, at any rate.

It was at Eli's earnest request that I visited his school one evening, nominally to attend a Renaissance discussion group led by Eli's departmental chairman, actually to promote Eli's tenure interests, which project I went at with all my heart, kissing fingers, doing my duties nicely, in the faculty common room till the meeting began. Though Eli still hadn't shown up, I was nothing dismayed, knowing I never need fear his bombing out at school, wherever else; knowing he never had, never would, dear God, not at school, even as, inexorably approaching from the far end of the corridor, came the hideously familiar snoring and clunking as of a driven creature in leg irons laboring against all odds to reach the common room before he died. Don't let it be him, dear God. Dear God, if it has to be him then, don't let him mow down the stack of chairs by the door, proceed regardless to join the circle, seat himself stertorously beside me, keel over, a dozen pills rolling out of his breast pocket and bouncing like marbles across the floor.

> *"Think of this, good peers,*
> *But as a thing of custom. 'Tis no other."*

You bet. Yet that indiscretion served him well in a way. Seizing the outside chance that he hadn't already dealt the coup de grâce to his prospects of tenure with that performance—not the meanest detail of which I forbore to acquaint him with the next day—thenceforth, limiting the observance of his custom strictly to nonworking days, he so redeemed his professional self as to persuade no less than the necessary two-thirds majority of his colleagues the following year to recommend to the college admin-

istration's albeit byzantine justice his permanent appointment. Small wonder either, for he was not only, by all
accounts, a superlative teacher when he was himself; when
he was himself he was simply the best company in the
world, the most perceptive and truthful, the most understanding of men.

In his final year to tenure though, he reserved all that exclusively for his colleagues and students. At home it went
by the boards utterly: not by way of drugs, for even at
home he bombed out seldom that year, and yet he was
never so far from himself. All that was large in him seemed
to wither: he had no time for anyone or anything not di-
rectly serving his tenure interests; no sympathy to spare for
those of our friends in like straits, nor any for those of
them already jobless, let alone for me who did have a job,
and a comparatively secure one at that. I just couldn't do
the job now, that was all, this pregnancy so sapping me.
What did I expect him to do about that? How should he
have foreseen, since I hadn't foreseen, when we timed this
pregnancy designedly to coincide with the school year,
to keep my indispensable pay packet coming without in-
termission, that I would flag so immoderately? I had a
constitution of iron, could always depend on that; didn't
doubt that I could go on running, pregnant and all, in the
same old way, once I got my second wind, once the first
week of school was over, the second week over, the third
then. All it took was an effort of will; and, indeed, all my
daily business amenable to such effort I could expedite.
But by no effort of will could I move my mind. Dragged
up by main force from where it lay sunk fathoms deep in
an unaccountable fantasy of my passing the months of that
pregnancy in the country, in a cottage with Poppy, garden-
ing, living off the land (though I'd never gardened in my
life, hated the country), it took compulsively to counting.

Fifty-four times already I had stood up in front of my classes mouthing inanities like a mechanical doll, forced to feign unawareness of what a disgrace I made of myself every hour upon pernicious hour, while the numbness, seated massively in my head, reached out from there and annexed my whole spirit.

I sat on the edge of the bed one school morning, fright gripping me like a straitjacket. The two hundred and thirty-six teaching hours still to go stretched out in a line before me to the crack of doom. Eli was dressing, wontedly soliloquizing meanwhile on the current state of his tenure prospects. Dully, from the uttermost depths of my desperation, I said, "I can't go on." As if it weren't on his express recommendation that I was increasing our family, as if I weren't pregnant for both of us, "If you can't, you can't," he dismissed me through gritted teeth, snapping in two the coat hanger he held in his hands.

What if he'd said—as he surely would have said up till this year—that I didn't have to go on, that he wouldn't have me go on, that we'd find another way? Maybe I could have rallied then, knowing he was with me, been able to bear my terrible disgrace at school, even perhaps not have felt it as such a terrible disgrace. It should never have come to that, anyway. It wasn't a long-established obsession. It was only of recent years that my job performance had come to matter to me as inordinately as if it were my only assurance that, despite Eli's inveterate reservations about me, I still amounted to something. But I couldn't so much as scrape by at the job now, I couldn't do it at all. "If you can't, you can't," snap. So much for me and my pregnancy, snap, except for a repeated reminder to the effect that if it were proving too much for me, as my incessant special pleading these days seemed to indicate, why, where could I better seek relief than at the abortion clinic? He wouldn't stand in my way, he guaranteed me that: I should feel free to choose.

I knew that didn't come from his heart, that he couldn't possibly mean it. He could challenge me safely, knowing he could always rely on me to take care of his heart of hearts' priorities, that I wouldn't go knocking on that door. Not there, no. Only where he himself always sought his relief I took mine. I took it, though always as secretly as if to conceal even from myself what my right hand was doing, but I took it every teaching day of those early months, because it did do the trick. If it didn't sharpen my job performance, it did take the edge off my consciousness of my ignominy, enough, anyway, to enable me to go stumbling on—knowing nothing, not permitting myself to know anything, except that I had to go on.

The fatigue never let up, but by the turn of the year, with the first half of pregnancy behind me, my head began to thaw out; and then in spring Eli's parents came to my rescue. Longing sorely to see Poppy, they sent us the needful for Eli to fly to Los Angeles with her, leaving me the full week of the mid-semester break just to stay home in bed and stare at the ceiling to my heart's content. Gratitude spurred me on to transcend my exhaustion, to trim ten pounds off Eli's frame for their sakes. But the night before he and Poppy were off I woke in the small hours tossing and scratching in a bed so thick with crumbs I might have been sleeping under the rich man's table. Bombed out and bloated, the ten pounds restored to the last ounce, Eli requited me, and with such a vengeance as fully manifested itself only when, having seen them off at the airport, rejecting Poppy's recommendation to shake hands with him and be friends, I returned to find in our bathroom the doors of both cabinets swinging wide, their shelves bare, every single one of his dozens of vials gone with him, to rampage on, or not, no matter, the message was plain. Doubled up, howling like a dog, I could not have been struck at harder if those swinging doors had been Eli's own foot swung in my teeth. And I wasn't over it either when he called to announce their safe arrival; called again a moment later to beg my pardon; and again to ask if we were friends, if I loved him; and again, howling for mercy. But I was over it by the fifth call. And over it, over it all two months later with Toto's birth; and so was Eli. His long ordeal, his state of suspense, bedeviling, denaturing him, all over by then, Eli was himself again. Toto and I came home to a spotless apartment filled with the scent of flowers; and for those brief weeks that that little son, little brother, was with us, such was the bliss he crowned us with that Eli, as tenureless, prospectless, as he was by then, was to recall them for long long afterwards as the happiest weeks of his life.

CHAPTER
Six

We went to ground for the year after Toto's death with my folks in England. I was helped, I was fortunate. Money presents came pouring in then, so I didn't have to be back at work, as my colleague McNulty did, right away, meeting the world every day as if he weren't living in an inverted order. It was midnight, a mid-August midnight, when the call came from the hospital for Eli and me to take up our stand for the last time beside that bed where our son had lain for a month of days, getting smaller and smaller, till all that was left of him now was this minute skeleton, eyes open, burnt out; his mouth, unfastened at last from the breathing tube, stretched wide, the bare infant gums exposed, baby of mine. So he parted from us.

"But I didn't kiss him good-bye," Poppy said, when we broke the fell news to her the next day. We did though, for her, some hours before he was cold altogether; kissed the little head that was still warm, though death was visibly upon it. Poppy said, "You know Sai Sai, Mama? Sai Sai's missing Toto"; said, "You know Alison, Daddy, I want to go to Alison's house to tell her Toto died"; said, "Will you get me another little brother, because I'm missing little brothers." Meanwhile, from my overseas kin, Mama at the helm, a strong pull and a long pull and a pull all together, came exhortations daily to make tracks for England, hole up there for the year. I wouldn't have to be back at school again then; I could just sit. Eli said it was too lonely in our house without Toto, anyway. So I put in for a year's leave of absence; and Eli chose freely to cancel his terminal year at his school, the grace year his college administration had opted to favor him with in lieu of tenure. He said himself he had nothing to lose by it. But the day after he sent off his letter of resignation his hand shook so violently when he shaved that blood spurted from every inch of his face and streamed from his throat. And then he began bombing out again, so madly, and practically nonstop, that in sheer desperation, because it was unbearable now, I called Dr. Spinney for an appointment, though Eli had been out of his hands for the past year, we'd been so hard up, and he'd been on the wagon for tenure then, anyway. I proposed to consult Spinney myself now on Eli's behalf.

"I know you well, of course," he spoke first, "by hearsay." I could imagine, of the hundred-and-some hours that Eli had put in there, between those he spent on the nod and those he spent eating his heart out over tenure, how much of the time had remained for hearsay. "And I you," I replied, however, no less politely. In fact, except for observing once in a while that he always felt Spinney was on his side, all Eli had ever said about him was that he was without exception the most extraordinary-looking man he had ever seen anywhere in his entire life. Once, when Eli was too far gone to get there on his own, I'd taken him there; but he'd got the day wrong or the hour wrong, so I didn't get to see Spinney that time. Another time, Eli, glimpsing him getting out of a cab on a neighborhood block, flew to fetch me to take a squint at him, but too late, Spinney had vanished, so I didn't get to see him then either. And now that I did I had no heart for it. He certainly was unusually tall and thin, and he certainly did have a tentative face. Tentativeness was not what I would have expected in the face of a latter-day soothsayer. Shifting my eyes with difficulty from my dancing hands to his tentative face, it was Eli I'd come to see him about I said, hurriedly, before he took me for a prospective patient. I told him Eli hadn't got tenure, that he was bombing out almost daily now, that our son—we'd sent him an announcement of Toto's birth —our son was dead.

He bent swiftly towards me, his face flooded with concern so pure and so intense that for a moment I was electrified. Then he said, "Have you cried?" cupping his hands over his eyes in a vivid little gesture as if catching their tears. "Have you *cried*?"

What sort of question was that? What about Toto's crying? We never heard that at all the last three weeks of his life: the breathing tube down his throat took his voice away. Only now that his suffering was over I seemed to hear him crying out night and day against it, crying, little man, till the end of the world.

"What are your feelings about it?" Spinney was asking now. "How do you *feel*?"

In the corridor, outside the intensive care unit, where we used to wait mornings and evenings for the doors of the ward to open, a young man in a wheelchair, his right leg amputated above the knee, was always riding there, back and forth, nonstop, incessantly on the lookout to waylay any passing doctor, just to report, unvaryingly, every time he succeeded in collaring one, that he wasn't quite comfortable. He couldn't accept that the leg he'd lost was gone for ever. I feel like that. I feel the same as parents bereft must always feel; and must always have felt, despite the opinion of one of the nurses on Toto's case that Eli and I would surely have been better off in the old days of large families when losing a child in infancy was a matter of course. As if the peculiar tenderness the naked newborn babe inspires in us these days wasn't in force then, because they had such large families. And did the dying baby suffer less too in those days, because there were so many of them? And these days, do Third World parents suffer less, because where they come from forty of every hundred children born die in infancy? I never walk the streets now but I think of the thousands of thousands like me walking the streets of the world, not knowing how they're ever going to make it home.

"I feel blighted," I said. But that isn't what matters. He will never bend to smell the rose, his heart will never leap up at the sight of the rainbow. That's a fact, not a feeling. The fact is what matters. Only that, the fact of itself, is what matters. "But about Eli," I returned to my errand, "bombing out again, worse than ever, much worse."

"The wonder is," Spinney marveled cheerfully, counting my blessings for me, "that he's still alive." But as for what I should best do to keep him alive, "Stand by him," that was all·he came up with. Stand by him, while his two hundred pounds of solid bulk crash-landed against me every day. Still, I remembered Spinney in the ill year to follow, not for his counsel—anyway, it was Eli, as it turned out, not I, who did all the standing by that year—I remembered him just for the look he gave me when I told him our son was dead.

We took off for England soon afterwards, in the early fall, the three of us, and though golden and windless the afternoon of our departure, like fugitives from a tornado, huddling together. We went to England with only one plan

in mind, and set to it there indefatigably, Eli and I, poring
over my temperature chart every day; every month's end
laboriously discovering reasons for the greater likelihood
of the next month's success. I made secret wagers, new
ones for each new week, each new month. That single apple hanging from the bare tree outside our kitchen window, if it does not fall this week I will conceive; if it does
fall this week I will conceive. I will this month because this
is my birthday month, this month because this is my sister's, this my daughter's, my mother's. I will because I
must, because this month we timed it right, because the
fertility pills will work this month, because they must.
The Harley Street doctor said they were explosive—five,
six babies all at one birth. I had names for them all, a secret list prepared for our unconceived progeny whom we
strove for so hard, lying there together, tears of anguish for
the irrecoverable son, of desperation for the unconceivable
son, bursting like shot through our lids.

Drugs contraindicated in pregnancy, Slansky had told
me; drugs contraindicated in pregnancy, the Harley Street
specialist bore him out, would account for the child's fatal
heart defect, had I taken such drugs. I made no admissions,
but betaking myself in secret to the medical literature, I apprised myself of the facts, all the latest findings in that
field. What margin of reasonable doubt they allowed for
was too narrow to take refuge in. I told no one, not Eli nor
anyone else, what I'd learnt, what I'd done. My unequivo-
cal consciousness now of what I'd known all along really,
anyway, made no difference that mattered. Only the stuff
of my fantasy was all that was changed. No more recreating Toto's first month, having Feffer detect the trouble at
birth, the pediatrician diagnosing it right, ourselves seeking a second opinion at once, the moment he took to that
butterfly breathing, before he went into heart failure, in

time to save him, save him. No more of that kind: instead, an unending train of thick-coming fantasies recreating the early months of that pregnancy, myself just walking into my chairman's office, just telling him I wouldn't be back till spring, just telling Eli, without apology, invulnerable, unafraid, that I'd taken off school for that term. "Don't look sad, Mama," Poppy would momentarily penetrate my brown study, "don't cry," though I wasn't crying, "just wait and see, we'll get us another baby brother, and this one won't die. No more baby brothers to die, right, Mama?"

It was mid-winter when I did my researches. For five months I kept my countenance; but when the anniversary of Toto's birth came round and still there was no sign of compensation, then I told Eli. "I sabotaged you," he said, first thing. Then he said, "For you it is less unendurable to impute the cause to your own doing than to an accident of Nature beyond your control." He said we must air ourselves, seek diversion, travel. We had money enough for it, we were loaded. So we traveled all summer, first in Greece, sailing from island to island; and tried in our cabin, and tried in our room in every taverna we spent the night in, even with Poppy sleeping there, tried to conceive. I had no other purpose, no other interest. My temperature chart was my only study. I looked unmoved at the lovely terrain beneath those blue skies, and unmoved at the works of art and the people. But when I looked at Eli whom I had robbed of his son, hand in hand, always, with Poppy whom I had robbed of her brother, it was a torture to me. For the longest time I stood watching a legless beggar in Athens, propelling himself down the street on pads, effortfully, determinedly living, wanting to live. Surely a shining example for those of us walking in darkness; but not for my taking, not without getting my heart's sole desire, no way. Nor did those women I watched in Jerusalem at the Wailing Wall, tucking between its stones their supplications in writing to the Almighty to make them fruitful, stir up any atavistic impulse in me to follow their lead. Is God a man, that he should repent? For them their prayers and their begging letters; for me my calendar, my thermometer, and my temperature chart.

So our furlough year passed and was over, and I was not saved. Back on home ground again, all back to school again: Poppy to kindergarten; Eli to teaching where he could find it, at the lowest rank now, for a pittance, while he studied at night the doctrines of psychoanalysis, turning his mind—perhaps with the cure of his own little bunch at the back of it—to that discipline for his new profession, his old one being quite done for now with the job market's closure. Back to school for me too, no help for it. The gods had already amply tempered their justice with mercy; my punishment was not to be greater than I could bear. I had had a year's respite to lie down under it. Up now and walk, forward to the next class and the next and the next, to replay there, hour upon leaden hour, the same old scene, but with no little life to imperil now, no choice to make. I had made the choice here twenty months ago; was bound to it now, the stake of my *hamartia*; was become its personification, at once pride and pride's punishment; still toiling, incessantly, vainly, against impossible odds, to save my face. Onward across the campus, forcing my stiffening legs to go on, go on, on and on, till that distant day when, still on my feet, I would stop at long last, a fixed figure there, turned entirely to stone.

It was not that I couldn't go on, not that I couldn't bear it now: I could go on, I could bear it; but half of my classes were already mutinous, the rest thinning out as if pestilence-stricken. My job was in jeopardy, and there were Poppy and Eli, their heads to keep a roof over till Eli was qualified. To this end, seeking only, so I assured myself, the

minimum relief to restore the minimum competence necessary to safeguard my job, I called Dr. Spinney for an appointment, and dragged myself there at the end of the
week.

Spinney said, "It is the truth we are concerned with
here," as if it were in the cause of truth that he sought to
lay Toto's defective heart at Nature's door instead of at
mine. Eli had tried a much finer-spun argument, and I
hadn't been moved by his sophistry either. I hadn't come
seeking placebos for guilt. I had done my research. There
was evidence and no doubt. Sole author I, sole cause.

But research aside, how else, Spinney asked, had I spent
the year?

Mourning.

But what else had I done?

I had done that full-time.

But had there been nothing to distract me, nothing that
whole year to take pleasure in?

Once, in London, with Eli and Poppy, driving through
Regent's Park, back of the zoo, the sudden, amazing sight
of two giraffes, their massive, noble necks with the tiny
grotesque heads atop silhouetted against the wintry sky.
Look, Poppy, God's creatures! "Once, in London," I told
Spinney dully, "I saw two giraffes."

I was interested in animals then?

No, not at all, never gave them a thought, except that
whenever I'd encountered them, giraffes on the road, hip-
popotamuses on the river, it had struck me happily that
they lived in this world too and shared it with us.

"You have encountered them often then, have you, hip-
popotamuses and so forth?"

Their rounded backs above the river's surface, in their
element, how lovely I'd thought them then, with what
pleasure since then I'd recalled those scenes. But I couldn't
remember the feeling now, just remembered I'd felt it. I

said, "On my way home through Africa, I encountered them often."

He picked up on Africa. He had gathered from Eli—he hoped he wasn't betraying a confidence—that I'd been politically active in Africa. What about my political interests now? What newspapers did I read, for instance?

As if newspapers were any index of what was going on in the world.

Did I watch TV then?

I had once in England last year—the Yom Kippur War on newsreel—just a couple of months after Toto's death, those months in which I saw through and through, with intolerable clarity, whatever my eye chanced to light on; saw the strings directing the movements of the young men mowing one another down; saw the puppeteers offside, invisible to the normal eye, manipulating tribal feelings for ends diametrically opposite to the good of those young men mowing one another down.

Was there nothing at all I was interested in then? "What about your daughter?" he seemed to reproach me. "Are you a good mother to her?"

Even in the thick of my listlessness something grated. "What is a good mother?"

Indeed hard to say. "Are you a feminist?" he asked tentatively.

What did I care about that now? But I supposed I had to say something. Without interest I quoted Trotsky: "In order to change the conditions of life, we must see them through the eyes of women"; but felt bound to add, in all conscience, that I had never thought of the eyes I saw the conditions of life through as the eyes of a woman particularly.

"You feel you see things more in the way a *man* sees them, do you?"

"Woman's way, man's way, to tell you the truth, I don't

see things any way these days, can't take anything in, or give anything out. I can manage all right, except for my job. I'm not in quest of a panacea. Just so as I can keep going at school, without seizing up in the classroom in front of my students, that's all I want help for, nothing else."

He said he was sure he could help me in my trouble at work, and perhaps in other areas too where libido was likewise inhibited.

I shuffled home, straining in unabated agony through the next seven days, till my appointment with Spinney came round again.

Dreams in the interim?

Yes, I'd dreamt all our plants had died.

So we had plants in our apartment? I was interested in plants then?

No, I wouldn't say interested.

He racked his brains. I had, as he recalled, mentioned Trotsky last week. Trotsky was one of his chief and abiding interests. He had been with the Trotskyists once, you know.

Had he indeed? So had I, so had I.

And where did I stand now?

Ah, I was no longer politically active, hadn't been active for quite some years now.

So I had broken with the revolutionary Left then?

No, I wouldn't say *broken*. I hadn't changed sides. I held no brief for the light-that-failed persuasion. I hadn't gone over to the enemy camp.

"I know what you mean," Spinney nodded. "You remain rightly critical of the system, but you've come to feel we should make sure we're getting a better one before we give up what we've got."

"Who is *we*?" I barked.

Had I not, he had meant, been repelled in the end, as he had been, by the totalitarianism of the Marxist Left?

I said, "Even if that were the ground of my quarrel with them, the facts they look in the face remain facts no less. The truth does not change because I have changed."

"What facts? What truth?"

"Capitalism is murder," I said, astonished to hear my voice shaking as with a live passion.

For a long moment Spinney was perfectly silent. Then, "You are very unusual," he said quietly. The hour was over.

I walked effortlessly to the bus stop, was there before I knew it. You are very unusual, he had said. Though I had sat there, nobody, heavy as stone, still Spinney thought I was somebody. Very faintly, like the first faint drip that heralds the thaw in the icebound regions, something moved in my ice-locked interior. A particle of my mind was freed to entertain itself again. From that moment I began to recover. For minutes on end that week I thought of Spinney; and as I counted the hours of each day, and each day of that week away, I was not merely counting them away to count another week away, I was counting forward to Friday that was Spinney day.

I had not looked at him hitherto with seeing eyes, but looking now with heartfelt interest I saw how strangely and wonderfully he was made. A seven-foot cadaver: no trunk to speak of, no stomach at all; two-dimensional, no depth to his body, wouldn't last out a week in a concentration camp. But the comparative solidity of his great stooping shoulders was reassuring: all the rest—yards upon yards of arms and legs as thin and brittle as uncooked spaghetti—depended on them. Sparse gray hair clipped short atop his long skull; face very clean-shaven; his whole person, in fact, spotless as fleshless, seemed framed in an am-

bience of hygiene, like a cordon sanitaire. A kindly face in
its way, with great wary shadowed blue eyes, faintly red-
rimmed, deep-set in their cadaverous sockets. Nothing
dangerous in his face. If I'd been hitchhiking in a deserted
region, I would have accepted a ride from him without a
moment's hesitation, if he'd offered me a ride. A broad
gold ring on his left hand showed how married he was.
One could well understand what his wife saw in him,
with his ostrich legs leading off from his armpits, and his
kindly, tentative face, and his winsome smile.

When I told him I was better he gave me a special smile,
as big as the world, that went on and on till I thought,
Enough already, smile and have done with. But at the same
time I saw in his smile how enchanting he was when the
blood came to his bloodless face and his blue eyes shone,
what a beauty he was.

"Well, now," he said, "we can begin our real work." He
leaned towards me confidentially. "In the two years or so
since Eli was in treatment with me, you know, I've been
specializing in sex."

No accounting for tastes in specialization. Tabulating
the hundreds of ways, no doubt, each on its own spotless
index card. But I assumed an expression of interested ap-
proval.

"Does talking about sex embarrass you?"

I never talked about it. What was to talk about? Those
who can do, those who can't talk about it.

"But you do have a good sexual relationship," Spinney
urged nonetheless, "with your sexual partner."

Why didn't he say with Eli? A rule of the profession, no
doubt, to refrain from naming names in this context. But
the anonymity chilled me; the language made me altogether uneasy. He was eyeing me keenly. I must be looking
uneasy. I wished we could return to the subject of our dis-

cussion last week. He had been a Trotskyist, he had said. I had so much in common with him already.

He recalled me abruptly. "What turns you on?" But as I goggled at him, speechless, "I mean what movies, what books turn you on? *Lady Chatterley's Lover?*" he helped me along.

"Oh, *that* isn't DHL's great work," I replied in a rush. I was so relieved. For a sickening moment then I'd thought he was pressing me for the highlights of Eli's lovemaking. "*Sons and Lovers* and *The Rainbow* now, those are his great works."

Yes, Spinney said happily, the other was hardly the definitive work on sex. "I think I can safely say," he went on to assure me without a qualm, "that I know more about sex than D. H. Lawrence." To such a pass had his specialization brought him.

"Let alone knowing *more*," I replied at once and with perfect confidence, for I was on firm ground here, "than Lawrence knows about any aspect of human relationships, you know not one iota of what Lawrence knows."

But I had misunderstood him. Of course he didn't claim to know more than Lawrence, an artist, a genius, about human *relationships*. Sex was what he had said, that's all.

"Isn't sex a human relationship then?" Did I smell a rat?

"Now you're twisting my words." He was a mite reproachful. "I'm a scientist. The artist has his appropriately artistic approach, the scientist the scientific-analytical approach. Surely, with your Marxist education, you're familiar with that. But we mustn't," he forestalled my reply, "lose track of our subject. We were ascertaining, remember," he smiled quizzically, "that you do enjoy sex." He lingered long on *enjoy*, savoring it. How at odds his plummy accents were with those austere lips that shaped them. "You enjoy it, you look forward to it." Snug in his vacuum-packed candyland specialization, sealed off from the past, insulated against the charged heart, uncontaminated by love or rage or grief or despair, he sat back awaiting what I had to say.

I told him I was trying to conceive.

"And you enjoy it, do you then, when you try to conceptualize?"

His clanger, not mine; but he claimed that I had prompted it in him. "You intellectualize your feelings," he said, "when what I want from you is just the *raw* feeling," making a cup of his great shapely hand to cradle the raw feeling in.

I said, "I just want my baby back again, that's all." Was that raw enough for him?

He bent at once towards me, so intimately it was as if he were holding my hand. "If I were to lose one of my own two children," he said with momentary blazing intensity, "I would hate my life. But I'd live it," the tension slackened, "for my other child, for my wife," his voice trailed away, "for my patients."

But I carried that moment of understanding away with me—"I would hate my life"—and warmed myself with it all through that week.

I got through that week, and the next, and the next, because there was Spinney to talk to, to talk to me, for an hour at the end of it. I would get there way ahead of time, walking round and round the block for an hour and more in the dead of winter, to be there on the dot, so I wouldn't lose one moment of that hour that was my reward for each week's travail. So I got through the weeks of that semester. If I dragged myself in irons, I was not locked into them so strictly now. If I walked on nails across the campus, they were not there now every time I crossed it, not there on Friday, the day I saw Spinney. One night after school, toiling up the steps of the subway, I looked at the token booth at the top—the portcullis between my two lives, my two worlds—and I thought, No one else looks at that token booth with my eyes. And what that meant was that the consciousness that was mine was stamped distinctively as mine; and I felt that in myself as a thing of value.

I could look at Poppy now not only as the child whose little soul I had dealt an irremediable blow, I could look at her now with an iota of pleasure, play with her, tell her stories, without its being an extreme exertion. I could read again. I had something of a life now to share with Eli, began to share his with him again. I was glad to see my friends; I could teach again without fear, talk to my students freely, all because Spinney had freed me to do so. I knew he had not reclaimed me on purpose, that he didn't know how he'd done it; but as if he had harrowed hell for my sake, I worshipped that man. And though I entertained few illusions about his moral—and as few about his intellectual—rectitude, there was nothing he could say that did not seem to me most fit to be pondered. When I displeased him I lived only to make up for it at our next appointment; when he smiled, when I appeared to have given the right answer; when he seemed to be warming to me; if he gave what I could interpret as a little sign that he liked me, I carried that with me through the week like a talisman.

CHAPTER

Seven

The very day after we had returned from our year abroad, as promptly as I, hotfoot on the old fertility trail, was at Feffer's office, Eli, at the adoption agency, was filing an application for a Vietnamese war orphan, those being soonest obtainable. The social worker assigned to our case duly interviewed us, first together, then separately.

"So you lost a child last year. Well," she looked up from our application papers, "are you over it yet?"

I looked out of the window. "Pretty much over it."

In the line of duty she paid us a house call. About our suitability as adoptive parents, she told me aside then, she had only one reservation, specifically about me, whose eyes, she had noticed, when I'd claimed I was over my son's death, had wandered. I'd better get this straight: the baby we'd be adopting would be, in the first place, no duplicate of the one we'd lost; in the second place, not that much of a baby. What they'd got us down for was one who had survived his first year—which wasn't to say he'd be healthy, but made him a safer bet than the nurslings. We couldn't afford to be losing another child, right? To us both she said in departing, "Our agency doesn't believe in the wholesale assimilation of the child's native culture to the adoptive parents' culture, so you're going to have to Vietnamize the household."

"Like defoliating the plants," Eli shrieked, "napalming the rooms, dragging in the United States Army?"

But when, six months later, by which time, *mutatis mutandis*, Cambodia's war orphan production rate was outsoaring the rest, we were notified that a fourteen-month-old Cambodian boy, particularized by a name and a birthdate, had been earmarked for us, Eli jumped to it. Up to his eyes in Cambodian culture, with Poppy he pored over pictures of Angkor; he read her Cambodian fairy tales; our rafters rang with recorded Cambodian folksongs on such themes as the breasts of the giant's daughter, big as guitars.

But whereas, weeks before we set eyes on the child, Eli made him his son and Poppy's brother, such thoughts as I gave the little scrap still hanging out in the orphanage in Phnom Penh did nothing to detach me from my thermometer—still my sole index of hope for the future; nothing to stop the crying I still woke with most mornings, as if that were what my eyes opened for—crying as I sat on the edge of the bed to dress, as I filled my coffee flask for school at the kitchen sink, and went on my way still crying, because, though it wasn't a bottomless black hole that monopolized all my sights nowadays, still I saw no hope. It was Eli who did all the hoping: making himself a new heart, a new spirit, in the teeth of my hopelessness, he made us a future. God knows, I had reason to bless him for that.

But it drove me mad when, as it seemed to me, he overlooked the cost, so mad that one leisurely morning, when —bethinking himself of our year in England, and dwelling with reminiscent pleasure on our summer travels—he expressed some regret that we hadn't traveled more, hadn't spent the year altogether more fruitfully, I flew at him with violent hands to enforce his remembrance of what had occasioned our furlough that year. Bare hands weren't enough. Advancing upon him with bread knife and chopper, I pinned him to the bed, put the knife to his forehead, drew blood. "Like a samurai," Eli said afterwards, "with all that equipment." But he took my point, as he always did these days.

The whirligig brought in its revenges promptly. I was assaulted myself that very week, by a woman too. She came bulldozing at my back, mowing down all before her, on the stairway down to the train in the morning rush hour. I managed to elbow her fleetingly in the ribs as she passed. That did it. She was waiting for me on the platform where the train was still standing. Hanging on to my hair as I flung myself through the closing doors, roaring her vilifications forth, she beat me over the head with a hand of iron for the space of two stops. It was not for me to try conclusions with her in a crowded train, nor did any of the commuting citizenry come to my aid, though one did think to tell me, when my assailant had at last spent herself, that a contact lens was stuck to my cheek.

I entertained Spinney with an account of this episode at the end of that week.

"Was she black?"

Should she not be black? Whence came the bulk of the violence in this city but from the most violated of its citizenry?

"Yes, but how did you feel at the time it was happening?" Smilingly intercepting my answer, "I think I can guess what you're going to say." His smile, his intimate little assurances that he knew me, and so well as to predict my responses, always warmed me.

"I'm sure you can guess," I agreed delightedly. "All the while she was savaging me, I was thinking, This is what Eli must feel like when I savage him—this mortal shame, this ghastly humiliation."

Flunked again. A shamefaced admission of racist feelings was what I'd been cued for. And why? Because such had been the feelings of another woman patient of his— very liberal, active in civil rights and so on—in a similar pass. And such, therefore, my hard-earned political education regardless, should have been my feelings too.

Those other women patients of his—never a shining Spinney hour passed of late without his improving it with now one, now another, example of their uniform and un-relieved inanity for my emulation. His other women patients demonstrated their recovery from depression by taking a renewed interest in their appearance, going shop-ping for clothes, experimenting with new hairdos, new makeup, shaving their legs. "It can be very moving," he rebuked my retching, "to see a woman showing an interest in life again by shaving her legs."

But he wasn't moved by seeing me take an interest in life again by reading, disputing. Not that he was averse to in-tellectualism in his women patients, by no means. But if any other of his intellectual women patients in deep dis-course at a faculty party with a visiting mediaevalist were to be abruptly cut short in mid-disquisition by the visiting scholar's inquiry as to whether she wouldn't rather be in bed with him, why, she, far from being mortally af-fronted, would relish such an inquiry as a compliment to her femininity, a welcome reminder to her that she was a woman. When his other women patients had their differ-ences with their husbands, he was telling me now, they expressed their anger appropriately, by weeping, for in-stance, and expostulating. No doubt Eli had given me cause to be angry, but did I not think my anger excessive?

No, I didn't. Sometimes I thought it was only anger that kept me going at all.

"But you've told me yourself repeatedly how hard he tries these days, what a changed man he is. Now why can't you rejoice at that?"

"Rejoice? As in the Lord? I can't, because we had to lose Toto, no less, before Eli got wise. The memory of those tenure years eats my heart away. As considerate as he is of me now, I'm still unable, I'll never be able to forgive him for those years."

"But that man was in agony in those years." Spinney took up the cudgels, ostensibly on Eli's behalf, with sanctimony so icy I perished. "Couldn't you understand that? Have you no idea what it is for a man under threat as he was of losing his job, his livelihood, the means to supporting his family?" Then, his voice softening, magnanimous Spinney, bending over backwards to see it my way, "But he didn't consider your *needs* sufficiently, he didn't *help* enough, is that it?"

"The one time I told him I couldn't go on," I choked out through the great tide of grief and rage, black and bitter as hell, that charged my throat, "he just said, 'If you can't, you can't.'"

"If you can't, you can't," Spinney repeated, carefully uncomprehending. "So? What was so bad about that?"

Eli himself had told me since then what was so bad about that. He'd told me himself that he'd sabotaged me. But I couldn't say so to Spinney. My mouth was full of ashes.

"Of course," Spinney recollected, "for you there was a child's life at stake, and a child's life, if not more important, is scarcely less important than a man's job." But hearing himself, he withdrew that at once. He hadn't meant to say that, hadn't meant that at all. His sympathy for Eli had run away with him for the moment. He felt an unusually strong identification with Eli, a special bond with him. "Eli's my sort, you see," he pleaded in that heart-to-heart way of his, warm as an embrace, "whereas you're not my sort."

So I wasn't his sort. That didn't have to mean he didn't like me, did it? I wasn't cut up at all. I knew he liked me, whatever the cumulative direct evidence to the contrary, knew he valued me underneath it all. He was just testing me. I thought, I'll just test him; and accordingly, just testing, wondered aloud at our next appointment if I shouldn't quit. How freezing it was in his office that day! He hadn't enjoyed these sessions, hadn't looked forward to them; I put him off, and he had a feeling that I put other people off too; I talked at him, not to him; his other women patients talked to him; they brought him sexual material; they came on with him as women; he didn't find me credible as a woman; I didn't strike him as a woman at all. One last word of advice: if I were intending to seek treatment elsewhere, he would urge me to choose, whomever else, a man, to work with me through my hatred of men.

I'd never noticed till now how like a duck's bill his nose was. Tolstoy said only unkind men had such noses. Please, dear duck's nose, don't let me go like this, as if all along I'd meant nothing to you. But he let me go, just like that. And I went, just like that.

That was the first time I quit him for good. I was back two weeks later. "To make a fresh start," Spinney suggested with feigned amicability, armed to the teeth with his petrified notions, idées fixes, moribund stereotypes— all suiting and serving, as suited and served by, his sexological enterprise.

No, I wasn't there to make any fresh starts.

"All well at home? Family going on an even keel?"

I wasn't there to discuss my family either.

My family, as a matter of fact unbeknownst to Spinney, now included in its membership a little brown boy we called Gilead, come twelve days ago on the last plane out of Cambodia, one of sixty starveling babies, all with running sores and running diarrhea, all alike exhibiting the standard effects of prolonged malnutrition. But there the likeness ended, for ours was not only far and away the pick of that bunch, he was a spectacular beauty by any criterion, only the medical one excepted. "Beautiful?" snarled the pediatrician we rushed him to—a black colossus, disgustedly scrutinizing our scantling couched commodiously in the palm of his hand. "Then find me some beautiful flesh on his bottom to give him a shot. In the hospital's where this eyesore belongs, except he doesn't have enough beautiful blood in his body to spare for their lab tests."

Home, Gilead spent his waking hours sitting up in his highchair in the kitchen, munching thoughtfully on his high-protein diet, deep in a brown study. "He's thinking about his mother," said Poppy. On the third day he reached a decision: breaking off a morsel of bread, he pushed it up one flat nostril, retrieved it, then offered it me with a smile—his first, and as dazzling a one as if his full set of mahogany-colored teeth had been pearls. From then on he moved fast, sounding the charge against Poppy, contesting, matchstick arms in full flail, brown nose thrust between us, her right to the merest kiss from Eli or me in his presence. "I wouldn't mind so much," Poppy observed with extravagant candor the day he fell sick, "if this one died." This one was not about to die, however. He had come incubating chicken pox. This one merely had chicken pox.

But Eli—his roving anxiety fastening upon this

chance—took fright and forthwith bombed out in his old style. I didn't respond in my old style though. I just said, Enough is enough, gave him cab fare to get himself to the hospital, bundled him out the door and double-locked it against him, till, half an hour later, cooled out, I went down to the lobby to fetch him back. But he wasn't there to be fetched back. He'd done just what I'd told him to do, to my horror; and they'd pumped his stomach and slapped him about and put him in the mental ward as a suicide case, treating him, as he told me subsequently, as if he were nothing—which punished me more effectively than the cruel pressure a whole committee of doctors put on me to let them keep him there. "If you take him out now," they promised me, "within a year he will be a dead man." But I signed him out, and took him home the next day.

An eventful couple of weeks; but it was not to report on Gilead's arrival nor on Eli's relapse that I was back at Spinney's, had to be back, be his odium never so insuperable, his benightedness never so impenetrable.

"About this alleged difficulty of yours in finding me credible as a woman," I took up the thread from where we'd left off.

Spinney readied himself. "You'd like to sort out your feelings about being a woman, is that it? Examine your conflict with your femininity?"

"With my what?"

"I haven't quite got the picture," making fast his blinkers, "of how you relate to men."

"Make the acquaintance of men, you mean, get to know them, make friends?"

"How do you make men see you as a woman, I mean?"

"I wear a pink bow in my hair."

"Do you never wear makeup," he paused delicately, "to enhance your appearance?"

"Never," I lied. In fact I always wore makeup, at all

times in public, had done so for years. I was wearing it then, to enhance my appearance. Why, Poppy had asked in the bathroom just that afternoon, was I making myself up so soft and pretty?

"No interest in what you wear either?"

Not, as a rule, your most studious dresser, admittedly, but what casualness I dressed with for Spinney was all of that studied sort, reportedly more bewitching than when art is too precise in every part.

"You don't want men to admire your clothes?" the un-bewitched Spinney pressed on.

"My *clothes*!" delivering my standard peroration on the trivializing effects of capitulation to physical narcissism and the ends it served.

"You want men to admire your *mind*, is that it? You feel your mind's your best part."

"I don't come in parts."

"No part of yourself you prefer to others? No part of your body you value especially?"

In fact there was. I looked fondly at my feet, those old troopers, that had walked me forth into the world, held me up in it, serving me in excess of duty at times, such as only a matter of days ago, at the hospital where Eli lay in a wretched huddle, imploring me to get him out of there, when, ignoring his plea, his trembling outstretched hand, I'd just said my say and turned on my heel and marched down the corridor to the exit, with every intention of leaving him there to rot, my feet of their own volition had swung me around at the exit, and marched me back to his bedside, and held me there till I took his hand and promised to bring him home that evening. My trusty, my intelligent feet. But even as I drew breath to say so, Spinney characteristically jumped the gun. "Do you admire your genitals in the mirror?"

Fending off an unwelcome image of Spinney admiring

his own in the mirror, "My feet," I said, launching instantly, before he could say foot fetishist, into the tale of
my earliest travels abroad, when, disembarked from the
Channel ferry, my redoubtable fellow-traveler and I, with
never a penny between us more, and sometimes less than
enough for subsistence, would take to the road all summer
long, roofless nights, hungry days no object, being pil-
grims bound for the shrines of art.

"You wanted to do everything a *man* could do, did you?"
Spinney weighed in, just asking.

Instantly the sunlit panorama in my head turned to soot.
I longed with a passion to push his teeth down his throat.
Why couldn't I just get up and out and have done with
the fellow? Why, in contempt of all reason, decency, self-
respect, did I have to return, keep returning to him, this
man of straw, who could only as he exceeded his mouse-
size measure of women assure himself he was a man at all?
Because that was not the whole story. Once, with four
little words, he had sprung the lock of my icy prison;
freed me to think thoughts, feel feelings besides those
that tortured me; told me he knew me for somebody.
"You are very unusual," he had said. Couldn't take it
though, not in a woman. But he was going to take it: that's
what I was back for, his mediciner, to make him take it.
If you are sick, as the Taoists say, go out and cure somebody. There was a special providence in Spinney's infir-
mity: it took my mind off my misery, concentrated it
wonderfully, battling with Spinney to work his cure. Not
that I got even such adventitious benefit free of charge.
First I paid him to cure me, now I paid him to cure him—
week in, week out, to toil up to my neck in the swamps of
his verbiage, viz.:

"But don't you find thinking, well, hard and thrusting?
Is there no place in your scheme of things for the open and
yielding?"

"How did your mother assert herself—as a woman, I mean?"

"Perhaps woman's new-found sexual emancipation will pave the way to her social emancipation."

Week in, week out, I was there on the hour, analyzing, exposing, exhorting, inveighing, bloodshot and hoarse, while he sat there opining in measured tones that the anger I saw fit to vent upon him was anger more justly due to my father.

Upon my father, that rock of integrity, for Spinney's rankness of soul, Spinney's unremitting baseness of mind, I should heap contempt on my father's head?

"How you do idealize your father!" Spinney crowed. "No wonder I never have quite got the picture of him, you mythologize the man so."

Notwithstanding which, full of professional dispatch, sparing no effort to get the picture, "He had a little car, did he, to get about in?"

I'd answered that one twice before already. Ask me another.

"Were there photographs, photographs of himself on the walls of his room?"

I got the picture of Spinney's father's room, and of Spinney's room—a double exposure of room upon room, plastered, wall upon wall, with counterfeit presentments of Spinney upon Spinney. "Working-class wages, where I come from, didn't buy fathers rooms of their own, nor little cars either, to get about in."

"Working-class?" Though he'd been with the Trotskyists once, you know, their heady polemics never clouded his judgment. He knew what he knew. "But the working class," the tip of his duck's nose ascendant, "has no taste, no discrimination." Pronouncing their doom, "They go in for direct sex."

Still, sometimes I thought I'd made headway. Once I was sure of it. I was telling him how, in my childhood, coming upon this pronouncement of Kipling's: "Now the reserve of a boy is tenfold deeper than the reserve of a maid, she being made for one end only by blind Nature, but man for several," as I idolized Kipling, how it had hurt me. And again, reencountering the passage, this time cited by a reputed critic as a prime sample of Kipling's sagacity, again the slap in the heart, because I knew as well then as now that deep-mindedness was the sovereign measure of human worth; and here was Kipling, whom I revered, pronouncing me *in aeternum* shallow-minded.

"But here you are, the living disproof of it!" Spinney cried.

The room spun madly around me. I heard trumpets sounding.

"He could never have said that if he'd known you," he went on.

I could barely restrain myself from kissing his hand.

"But what about your genital sensitivity?" he recollected himself. "There you have something that can be *scientifically* measured. That gives us something real to hold on to. After all, that's what matters."

I shook the dust—had there been any dust—of Spinney's wall-to-wall carpeting off my feet for five weeks that time. Then, from the bus that plied between his side and my side of town, because I was on the lookout for him, I saw him, exiting from the dry cleaner's on his block. Off the bus in a trice, I took up my post in the shadows to watch him wobbling along on his matchwood stilts, with one hand bearing aloft like a scutcheon his sterilized togs in their plastic sheaths, the forefinger of his free hand at his ear, gesticulating crazily, evidently addressing a spellbound audience, making his dazzling observations in quickfire succession, gabbling, smiling, delighted with himself. Spellbound I watched till he rounded the corner, out of sight; then gave chase, to pluck him by the sleeve, seize him by the lapel ("I will not let thee go, except thou bless me"); but pulled up short a couple of yards behind him, watching his gaunt back teetering up the steps and vanishing into his office building.

I called him for an appointment as soon as I got home. "But to what end?" Eli implored me. I'd been doing so well, I'd held out for so long. "You can't win them all."

All? As if I'd ever won any of them.

I dreamt I was standing some way from a house—a closed-up-looking house in a little valley in wooded country. In the house lay my mother, sick or dying. My own life was in terrible jeopardy. There had been a car standing in front of the house: it was gone now, and with it my hope of survival. Paralyzed with terror, I saw it returning down the hill towards the house; and as if that were a signal, all at once men by the hundred, armed with every killing device known to men—knives, ropes, shotguns, machine guns, guillotines, gallows, execution blocks— came pouring out of the woods. Men of every employment, every breed. You too, blackface, I thought. As they formed a circle around me, one man I observed in particular—a soldier in steel-gray uniform with gray hair to match. But then I saw that his hair was merely a gray cardboard helmet, and under the helmet only an adolescent boy. "Why, you're just dressed up as men," I declared to the whole assembly. Then as the circle closed in on me, "I'm sorry, gentlemen," I said with bitterest irony. Then at last, turning toward the house, "Mother, I'm sorry," I called from my heart, as they advanced in a body to kill me.

Identifying the soldier-boy without prompting from

me, "Yes, I see," Spinney said as serenely as if he had seen into the heart of my quarrel with him all along, and all along been entirely aware of its justice, "I can't be friends with a woman, and therefore I am not a man."

Ipse dixit. But though I waited, wise in the ways of this *ipse*, for him to unsay it, he didn't. Nor, when subsequently he said, "Your almighty respect for your father, that is what has sustained you through all your struggle with me," did he go on to mock that observation either. Not that the change in him could be scientifically measured, but it was enough to enable me, at the end, to go with my heart's enduring gratitude to him unadulterated by contempt. Still, it wasn't exclusively gratitude I remembered him with. He had burned me, not once or twice, but a dozen times, to the bare bone. I didn't forget that either.

Eight

A drawing of Poppy's, superscribed MY OWN DEAR FAM-
ILY, survives that period. There we stand, the four of us, in
a row: Eli, Poppy and Gilead, hand in hand, one indisseverable unit; I standing off, at the certain remove I kept
from them in those infirm years when who I was and what
I was living for I didn't dare to inquire. Toto lies prone in
his coffin offside at our feet. I thought then that Poppy, for
her part, had laid him to rest. I thought wishfully though,
as wishfully as I argued the other way, against her teacher's
misgivings, that, far from ominous, surely it was all to the
good that the lost little brother so freely announce himself
in her artwork and figure so large in her stories and conversation. Not she to repress it; observably she was working it out for herself her own way, my stalwart little girl.
Still, the fact remained, there was never a child so obsessed
with her health: the school nurse was sick of the sight of
her. And the fact remained that never these days, though
repeatedly certified sound as a roach, did she fail to bring us
new every morning dolorous report of her bodily symptoms,
till at last, herself locating their incorporeal source, she asked
Eli point-blank could he find her a children's mind-doctor.

Trauma, the children's mind-doctor said, indicating analysis, three sessions weekly, starting at once. Subject
to which, the prognosis was hopeful, outstandingly so,
Poppy being indubitably a loved child, the parental unit intact, and the patient herself independently initiating the
means to her cure. But what otherwise? If no analysis,
what about Poppy then? Not a pretty picture at all. Without the prescribed treatment, yes, her current symptoms
might well subside eventually, but only to give rise to
other more onerous symptoms. The cause would not dis-
appear. The child's mind was contaminated by death. That
was it then, straight from the horse's mouth. No more
construing it my way. I thought, This child too. God, let
me go already. I saw myself running, turning my back
on them all, on it all, just running nonstop, tirelessly, effortlessly, without end, onaway through the world.

He would have been four, pushing five by now, and she
blossoming, unscathed, had I run when the running was
good—that fall, if I'd left Eli then. No iffing about that;
never a ghost of a chance of that then; chance never entered
into it: I did not have it in me to leave Eli then. Now I do,
and to spare. Never mind how purposeful the change in
him these days, how heroic his labors to overcome his ad-
diction, to confront the wastes of his all-oblivious past, to
atone—even in the implacable face of my unforgiving-
ness—for his old unforgivable hardness of heart, it needs
only a word, and I'm leaving him. Let him merely, reflect-
ing with due compunction on the tenor of Poppy's early
years, groan, momentarily off guard, "What a toll they
must have taken of her, our rows!" and I'm on my way. It
takes only one to exploit, oppress and manipulate, bomb
out years on end, relinquish as by right his bounden duty,
propose in lieu of discharging same duty abortion of his
own progeny; but it takes two to tangle. *Our* rows. So

much for his penitential researches into lost years! Those who fail to know the past are doomed to repeat it. So here we part, here I leave him, because what I sowed, in having continued to live with him then, is enough to keep me reaping full-time, enough destruction and desolation and ruin for me to answer for for the rest of my life.

But that's not all there is to be reaped, he would have me remember; I leave plenty out of the story too. Poppy is not lost, nor Gilead. Permanently bereft as we are, loss is not all we have to show for the years. We've got two living children; yes, and we still have each other too, he battles on: the deadly waters that rolled over us couldn't part us, not us. I wouldn't bet a nickel on that. But hearing how unweariedly he asserts this; watching him, his face intent, at attention, how its peculiar blend of innocence and experience deepens with these years of his becoming whom he was meant to become, I turn back from the door.

So it goes, sometimes with a spell of calm so prolonged that I take to thinking myself done with bitterness at long last, its indurate fossilized core quite dissolved. Not so fast. We wait at a bus stop one night, homeward bound after a movie. I haven't stood at this stop in five years. That fall semester when I was teaching evenings, a colleague sometimes gave me a ride this far, then here I'd wait, counting dully, on the last lap home. Home to a tight-lipped Eli, cold-shouldering me, because my teaching schedule required him to be coping with Poppy those nights, on top of the load he had on his mind. What am I doing, still with him? What is it with me that I still haven't left him? He stands dazed, stricken, as I, erupting without a moment's notice, anathematize myself there in the street.

I'm not over it yet. I don't know that I'll ever be over it. But I hope I will. One can't live in the presence of hope, as I do—hope triumphant in Eli, incarnate in the children—

without its telling upon one eventually. But it's they, not I, who generate it. Hope doesn't well up in me as it used to, spontaneously, from an internal spring. That old well-spring can't be reactivated. Yet, even having established that, I can't swear to it. Mornings, waiting with Poppy and Gilead for their school bus, I have caught myself thinking, What will their memories be of their childhood? When they're grown up, what will they have to tell me about these years? I'm seeing myself in the future with them, looking forward unbidden. Where does that impulse come from? And lo, what partners it? No silver lining without its cloud. No sooner am I looking forward, set free to look outside myself, than I see the world's trouble, feel the imperiledness of this world more keenly than ever I did before. I have to contain this irresoluble contradiction too, make room enough in myself to accommodate all these oppositions, contrive to live with them all.

Here I stand with my children, dreaming about the future as if there certainly will be a future. There goes my brave Poppy—with what a hale future in mind for herself as a children's doctor, an animals' doctor, an artist, and a mother of six—propelling Gilead ahead of her into the bus. Gilead's vital concern just now is with bedrock matters. "You wanted a black boy, Dad? You wanted to get me? You wanted a boy like me, Mama?" A boy *like* him— our bright, particular star, little merry heart, wonder-working son of ours? "And him," Eli still says, still as incredulous as the first time he said it, "they would have thrown on to the rubbish heap!" Him, and her too. Our family is doubly connected to that rubbish heap. "Are these people relations of ours?" Poppy whispered, scrutinizing the frieze of photographs in Uncle Noah's backyard sanctuary when we visited there last summer. Only the photograph at the end of the row has no people in it—just two

words, written in Yiddish in blood on the wall of the corridor to the gas chamber. JEWS REVENGE, the words say.
What words, I'm thinking, as, waving the children good-
bye, I go down into the subway, forward to my school,
would I bite through the flesh of my finger to write on the
wall?

Out of the subway, into the bus, out of the bus, up
the street, through the gates, into the classroom. Into the
classroom, to teach the young things facing me there the
Sonnets again, as if the Sonnets save, as if that were what I
would write on the wall.